He was only supposed to help with the investigation, not be permanently transferred…

Taylor's mind buzzed with all the scenes he'd witnessed this day: the arrest of Peter Jurg by Lake and Olivar; the arrival of Suzanne Cooper, and then Evan Nichols on his bike; the drafty warehouse, chock full of paintings and props; and now this gallery, all silver and glass, and Glanz elegant and strange in his alluring suit and fierce hair style.

Glanz indicated a back room, olive in color, with a dozen cabinets to match. The tall cabinets each had six drawers, and Taylor estimated how many hundreds of files each would contain. Above the cabinets hung harsh, florescent lights. They crackled and conferred on the furniture a sanitized glow.

"The cabinets are not locked," Glanz said and left.

Taylor faced the staggering task, no help, no chair, and no knowing the consequences of not finding evidence of complicity in murder.

He found an A6 pad and ruled in columns for names and dates, while he wondered if he still had a post at Southwark. He begged to use the phone and learned from the officer on duty at Southwark that he, Taylor, had been seconded for the duration of the investigation.

"And aren't your ears burning, you filthy sod? And who the hell do you know at Scotland Yard, you skivvy prat?"

His insides kicked and his feet refused to move—for *duration* had the connotation of punishment. There'd be no early release from Nichols, no quick return to Taylor's regular slog, not for him, and not in the foreseeable future.

Taylor on Loan is told alternately by three protagonists—a British police officer, a Dutch investigator, and a forger's girlfriend. Each struggles to stay alive as police and criminals hunt them across Europe, finally colliding in a shoot-out on the docks of Dover. It's murder on everyone.

KUDOS for *Taylor on Loan*

In *Taylor on Loan* by Deirdre Feehan, Gareth Taylor is a British beat cop in 1980 when he discovers a dead man on the Blackfriars Bridge. Taylor is then loaned to the lead investigator on the murder case, and everything goes downhill from there. In the meantime, a forger's girlfriend and a Dutch investigator, both connected to the murder case, are on a collision course with Taylor in more ways than one. As the bodies pile up and the list of suspects grows, Taylor begins to wonder if his life will ever be the same. Well written, fast paced, and full of surprises, this one will keep you on your toes right to the end. A great read. ~ *Taylor Jones, The Review Team of Taylor Jones & Regan Murphy*

Taylor on Loan by Deirdre Feehan is the story of a man who only wants to do his job, earn his pay, and live a quiet life. Gareth Taylor is a British Bobby in December of 1980, walking his beat in Southwark, when he hears an accident on the Thames River and runs to the Blackfriars Bridge. There he discovers a boat has run into a scaffolding that should not be there—a scaffolding from which a murdered man is hanging. While this is fairly extraordinary in itself, it is nothing compared to the events that follow, turning poor Taylor's life upside down. Feehan combines stolen art, drugs, forgeries, missing money, and murder to create a chilling tale of intrigue, deception, and betrayal, making *Taylor on Loan* a worthy read that mystery fans should love. ~ *Regan Murphy, The Review Team of Taylor Jones & Regan Murphy*

Taylor
on
Loan

Deirdre Feehan

A Black Opal Books Publication

Black Opal Books

BECAUSE SOME STORIES JUST HAVE TO BE TOLD

GENRE: HISTORICAL MYSTERY/TRADITIONAL BRITISH

This is a work of fiction. Names, places, characters, and incidents are either the product of the author's imagination or are used fictitiously, and any resemblance to any actual persons, living or dead, businesses, organizations, events or locales is entirely coincidental. All trademarks, service marks, registered trademarks, and registered service marks are the property of their respective owners and are used herein for identification purposes only. The publisher does not have any control over or assume any responsibility for author or third-party websites or their contents.

TAYLOR ON LOAN
Copyright © 2018 by Deirdre Feehan
Cover Design by Jackson Cover Designs
All cover art copyright © 2018
All Rights Reserved
Print ISBN: 978-1-626949-93-5

First Publication: SEPTEMBER 2018

Published by Black Opal Books **http://www.blackopalbooks.com**

DEDICATION

To my agent,
John A. Ware (1942-2013)
and to my teachers
Michael Buckley
and
Lou Mathews

Chapter 1

Taylor

Government cuts put Sergeant Gareth Taylor outside, on foot, at two twenty-three a.m., Sunday morning, December 1, 1980. He descended the steps to St. Paul's Walk, deliberately noisy, giving any idlers and loiterers the impulse to move along. He wore the largest size police-issue boots, wide black coverings for feet that supported his six-foot-three-inch frame. He had reached that mark by age fifteen, two decades, one marriage, and two motorcycles ago.

For Taylor, the swirling fog had the taste of austerity. The chill seared his lungs as he breathed in the white, smothering river mist. His wool uniform grew soggy, chafing his skin as he moved.

Suddenly, there came a crash on the Thames, steel scraping the stone pillars of Blackfriars Bridge. A light popped, followed by alarms and human cries.

He bounded down the last two stairs, elbows out, and sped along the brick-lined walkway, vague in the limp beam of his flashlight.

The air's oily smell increased as he reached the overhang.

Caught in scaffolding under the bridge's hollow arch, a tugboat rocked. Its headlamp allowed Taylor to see the damaged vessel and the two boatmen who clung to the cabin. Above them swayed the body of a man in sagging clothes, dead at the end of a thick rope.

He waved his gloved hands, trying to catch the boatmen's attention. The captain yelled as horns boomed from a passing freighter. Decked in bright lights, it swerved dangerously close. The small tug fought and finally freed itself from the metal frame.

Slowly the boat inched its way toward the quay, toward Taylor who reached with open hands and caught the heavy thrown rope. On his knees, he looped it around the metal stanchion, pulled, puffing hard, bent double with the effort, straining against the icy winter air, and the weight of the craft yanking him forward. At last, it banged against the cement wall, and Taylor clicked his radio, calling in for help less than two hours after the start of his shift. His message was curt: not suicide.

He inspected the damage to the left side of the boat, his torch light illuminating the scrapes, scratches, cracks, and tears in the metal.

The captain and pilot, now safe, made complaints and demanded action, pointing at the bridge, the tug, themselves. They talked over each other, saying, "Who's going to pay for my boat? Who put that scaffolding there? It wasn't there yesterday. What workman would climb that? Look how it hangs over the water. Didn't anybody think about our boats when they put that right in the middle of the archway?"

All changed to sympathy when Taylor pulled out his notebook.

"Poor bastard," the captain said.

"Dead, surely, God help him," the pilot added.

Taylor peered at the swinging corpse, at the red-painted bridge and studied the angle of the crooked head; the bulging eyes; the ungloved hands; the cuffed, mud-spattered trousers and the shine of the one tasseled penny-loafer. The missing shoe bothered him. Did it fall? In the din, did he miss the splash?

He checked the lapping water, shining his torch in a slow arc, seeking the man's shoe. It seemed an important task to complete now in the raw, spatial present, with the body in view, the wrecked boat beside him, and the frightened men getting in each other's way in the small galley.

The pilot brought him tea in a tin mug. Drinking, he steadied himself against the tug's railing and spoke calmly to the fishermen shivering in their damp clothes. He bid them sit down and wrap up warm. He knew well that they would soon be fodder for detectives and gossip-peddling hacks.

He'd been stung by reporters pestering him on his beat with questions he couldn't or wasn't permitted to answer. He'd wanted to swat the one little bugger from Radio1 who kept shoving a mic at him last month, all because he, Taylor, had been at that Westminster pub bombing, and a word from a local bobby would really interest listeners.

Now he sat on the tug's rear bench, scribbling his record: the captain's and pilot's names, their boat's name, and their itinerary.

The sweet tea thick on his lips, he knew what upheaval this death would bring to his Southwark station: meetings, inquiries, paperwork, and overtime. The black waves slapped the side of the boat, disrupting his writing, the ink smearing on the moist paper.

He looked up at the rush of arriving officers, the

emergency workers staggering into St. Paul's Walk. They brought a frenzy with them and all their gear, latex gloves, steel cases, cameras, and lights.

Another camera flash blinded him. That made six in the last two minutes. He wanted peace to take the boatmen's statements. The captain and pilot huddled together, jamming their hands in their coat pockets and pulling their collars close against their necks.

Taylor bent his tall body toward the pilot, cutting off the press's view, his wet hair stuck to his neck. Blinking his eyes, he wished for a scarf to warm his head and ears.

When Commander Vernon Nichols strode in swiftly on short legs, his mackintosh buttoned close to the chin, with two younger officers in tow, Taylor stood up sharply. Suicide never brought out commanders to the riverside on a cold night. Only politics with international overtones required an entourage of panda cars and vans. Nichols meant Home Office, parliamentary inquiries, clandestine meetings, and cases requiring global cooperation. None of which Taylor had ever been involved in.

Taylor shoved his notebook into a pocket, awaiting the many questions to come. Nichols would lead the investigation, conduct the interviews, and draw the conclusions. Taylor would be thanked and returned to his beat, if he were lucky.

He knew the talk concerning this commander and his teams: Nichols was difficult, a micromanager, an overseer. People got killed working for Nichols. He left you in the dark. He ordered you out on idiotic assignments while he sat warm and dry in his office. Or, some said, in *your* office, going through your drawers and files until you were up on charges you couldn't even spell.

The lost shoe troubled Taylor less now. Nichols and his entourage worried him more. The tugboat captain and pilot scuttled away from Nichols, toward the undamaged rear of the vessel. They stared as if threatened. Nichols glanced at the forensic team, the little tug, and Taylor.

"Good evening," Nichols said, the Welsh accent slipping out.

Mumbled replies, eager nods, and an exchange of names followed. Taylor read from his notebook as instructed.

"Out here on your own, sergeant?" Nichols asked, stillness in his mule-deer eyes.

"Yes, sir," Taylor said, wondering if and when he would get home to bed. "We're shorthanded in Southwark these days. We've all had to take an extra shift, here and there."

Nichols's entourage had increased: two more senior detectives, a photographer, a driver, and four uniformed constables.

Nichols waved Taylor closer. "The men who found him?" Nichols nodded toward the boat, his eyes appraising him. "Good witnesses?"

"They'll confirm what I saw." Taylor leaned toward the small man, not mentioning the half-dozen skateboarders who had rattled out of the fog, taken their butchers, and then skated south in diamond formation. Taylor would catch up with them tomorrow, threaten them with parental notice, and they'd spill whatever they'd seen.

Nichols smiled. "I'm sure we'll get something out of them."

Then Taylor smiled, an automatic response, not a sign of equality or camaraderie. He pressed his fingers to his nose as he smelled the exhaust from a police boat clattering to a halt under the bridge.

The caustic mist made him cough, and the white lamps forced him to blink his eyes, making him wish he had read classics at university and taken a job in the health ministry.

Nichols turned from the bridge. "What brought you down here?"

"Making a tour of the quays, sir. Addicts shoot up in the alleys."

Nichols angled his head upward. "Look like suicide to you, Taylor?"

Taylor turned, watched the officers struggle with the body. "Hard for a person to hang himself from that scaffolding, sir. It juts out over the water. You'd likely fall in before you got the rope around your neck."

The officers put the body on a gurney, covering it with a sheet.

"Come along." Nichols waved to the man behind him. "Identification, Hines?" he asked a plump officer in a dark mac.

"British passport in his inside breast pocket, sir," Hines said. "William Terrence McIness. One Forty-Three Breckenham Court, Putney." Then he stroked his striped tie from its knot to its end, a finishing flourish to his report.

Nichols frowned, a deep glare visible even in the fog. "No wallet?"

"No wallet, no keys, no checkbook, sir." Hines frowned at Taylor with disapproval and establishing the pecking order.

"Detective Inspector Hines, Sergeant. Taylor." Nichols gave the men time to shake hands before continuing. "Tell Hines what you saw."

"Tall, well-dressed man, about forty, wearing a brown suit, no overcoat, no hat, no gloves, one shoe missing. Not dressed to go out, hanging from scaffolding he couldn't reach without a crate or barrel to stand on."

"Murder, then." Hines shielded his eyes from the stabbing lights and peeked at his wristwatch. The numbers glowed green.

"Sir." Taylor pointed at the bridge. "That scaffolding has been moved, or we'd have had accidents before this."

Nichols and Hines gazed at the now lighted arch.

"Hines, find out who installed the scaffolding and when. And get it taken down. We don't need more hazards on the river." Nichols turned to Taylor as Hines disappeared into the hive of police under the bridge. "You go with Sergeant Kitner to the Putney address."

Taylor swallowed, lowered his chin, so his spine lengthened. He breathed in the cold night air and the activity all around him.

He didn't want to leave. He wanted to take his normal place with the men busy on the walkway with the gurney and the blue and white police tape being stretched between lampposts.

But Nichols ordered him, and Nichols could make or break Taylor. That had to be remembered.

At his name, a younger man dashed to Nichols's side, bumping Taylor with a black umbrella. They shook hands.

"Snow expected tomorrow," Kitner said with a crow's smile.

"I hope I'm home by then," Taylor said into Kitner's ear.

"Examine his flat," Nichols said. "Call Putney Station and get someone to check the missing persons' reports. See McIness's description is distributed. You remember the address, Taylor?"

"One Forty-Three Breckenham Court, Putney, sir."

The distance from Southwark to Putney required a car, and a car had a heater, Taylor thought, wanting to be warm and dry.

Nichols started as noise came from Taylor's radio. "Then he threw the money on the Temple and went out and hanged himself," he said.

"Pardon, sir?" Taylor pulled out his notebook, pencil poised.

"Nothing, thinking out aloud." Nichols regarded the clogging traffic on the Thames. "I'll see the captain and pilot. Off you go." Nichols spoke sharply to Kitner. "Don't get lost."

The bow-legged Kitner led Taylor through clumps of arriving vehicles and purposeful, hurrying men to Kitner's car. Taylor followed calmly, happy to be away from the bustle and the dead man.

"Nichols a religious man?" Taylor asked, his legs squeezed into Kitner's Mini.

Kitner shifted gears and drove with abandon, his bony knees jammed under the dashboard. "Not particularly." His dark hair dripped from the mist. "Welsh, you know. Peculiar, poetic."

"You've worked with the commander long?" Taylor asked.

"If you think three years is long." Kitner checked the radio.

"And Hines?" Taylor looked at the door handle. "We had a cursory introduction."

"Henry?" Kitner sneered. "Can you believe that one? Henry Hines. Sounds like a news presenter, not the son of cop."

Taylor examined his knees. "Got a chip on his shoulder, has he?"

"No." Kitner leaned forward, his chest inches from the steering wheel, squinting and humming. "But every briefing starts with some bit of history that nobody else remembers. The great robbery of 'forty-four, the terrible murders of 'sixty-two. My father this, my father that. No end to his talk. Listen with one ear, if you listen at all."

The Mini's headlights barely pierced the darkness. Kitner rubbed the frosted window repeatedly with his sleeve. Taylor rolled down his window an inch to allow their breath to dissipate. The promised snow fell quietly.

Curiosity bit through Taylor's wariness. Metropolitan Police Commander, Vernon Nichols, called to this death, prepped and ready for that very duty. Had the Yard been looking for the man? Had Nichols been waiting by the phone for news of McIness?

These thoughts stirred Taylor, unaccustomed as he was to fanciful speculations. He stared at his watch with its reflective face. Already three hours spent waiting in that frosty wind and several more to daylight. He gripped the door handle as Kitner cut another corner close.

Kitner jammed the car against the curb. The long Putney street featured detached houses with brightly painted doors, slatted gates, brick porches and enclosed square gardens. But Taylor saw pruned roses bushes and thorny hedges standing bare and burnished by wind, with snowdrifts across rooftops, car tops, and dirty curbs.

They approached 143 Breckenham Court, steady in heavy shoes. A middle-aged man answered their knock. He balanced a bowl of cornflakes in his left hand and crunched a mouthful, milk visible between his teeth.

Taylor read from his notebook. "William Terrence McIness?"

"Never heard of him." The man shivered as if the chill morning air stabbed him through his dressing gown.

Kitner pushed forward. "May we come in?"

"I'm about to leave." The man raised his hand. "You stop right there."

Taylor noted the stockinged feet and the unbrushed hair. "Won't take long." He sighted over the smaller man's head and glimpsed a staircase with burgundy carpet and a carved, wooden banister.

"What's this all about?" The man stepped forward, blocking Kitner. "Where's your warrant card? I'm a solicitor. I know the law. I have a right to know." He stepped onto the porch and drew the door shut behind him.

"We've been given to understand this is the home of William McIness," Taylor said slowly, outwardly calming the glowering man.

"Well, it bloody isn't," the solicitor said. "This is my house."

"Mr. McIness's gone missing," Kitner said, and he wedged himself between the man and the closed door. "We were given this as his home address. Seen him lately?"

"I told you, I don't know the man." The man noticed the snow, looked back at his front door. "And I still haven't seen your warrant cards."

Taylor looked at Kitner. What did Taylor need with a warrant card? He was in uniform. Kitner pulled his card from his inside pocket.

"Your name, sir?" Kitner replaced his card in his coat.

"Hutchinson, Paul," he said. "Who's your superior, Sergeant? I'm going to file a complaint." He opened the door and balanced on the threshold, adding three inches to his height.

"Commander Vernon Nichols, Metropolitan Police," Kitner said. "Shall I spell it?'

Taylor caught a movement on the stairs. Someone else in the house? Wife, lover, friend? Taylor heard his stomach growl. "We've made an error. We've been given the wrong address," he said. "Please excuse us, Mr. Hutchinson."

"Your superior will hear from me." Hutchinson slammed the door.

Kitner walked toward the car, but Taylor hovered by the gate, not quite ready to quit this strange opportunity for investigation. "I heard someone. I want a look."

At Hutchinson's bay window, they watched as a woman, plump and tall, strode back and forward in a white dressing gown, yanking the belt tight. Hutchinson shifted sideways, his mouth moving. She pointed and jabbed. He concaved and his back arched—his bowl of cornflakes fell.

"He won't be getting any for a while," Kitner said.

Taylor smiled, in spite of himself, and remained quiet. His eyes narrowed, simultaneously observing one marriage and reviewing his own five years of marriage. He and Joan had never fought like that. He'd never feared her, never caved before her like a punched-in pail, never raged at her about a knock on the door, a cop on the stoop or a messenger. But then no one had inquired about a murdered man at his address.

Taylor's left foot slid forward, his boot splashed with slushy snow. Kitner grabbed his elbow. "What are you doing?" the younger man said.

"Wanted to know what that row's about." Taylor avoided the truth of his nosey-parker impulse to intervene and followed Kitner to the car.

Kitner gave an exaggerated shiver. "How about we get a move on?" He laughed as he slammed in the clutch with a great noise. "What a pair. Domestic bliss. You're not married, are you?"

Taylor shook his head, his lips lifting, imagining that white dressing gown slipping down Mrs. Hutchinson's backside to the floor.

"What's this about McIness missing?" Taylor asked. "He's dead. We just saw him hanging from a bridge."

"Had to say something," Kitner said. "You never know what people would blurt out. You get people off-balance, and then they say something stupid. You've seen that."

Taylor looked back at the house with unease. He seemed to lack some crucial information that Kitner, Hines, and Nichols all seemed to know. He tried to formulate questions about the murder and realized that he didn't know Kitner first name. "If you need to contact me later—" He angled his head to see both of Kitner's eyes. "—ask at Southwark for Gareth Taylor."

"Robert," Kitner said then gave an odd little wave with his right hand. "But please, don't call me Bob and don't make any jokes. Bob the bobby. I've heard them all."

Taylor bowed his head to hide his stupid grin. "Don't you address me as Sir Gareth. I've had my fill of Camelot and the Knights of the Round Table."

They laughed, admitting that they both hated their given names.

"Oh, and I'm the commander's driver," Kitner said. "This look like his Jaguar? You notice the spacious interior, the leather seats, the hand-crafted dashboard?" He smacked the Mini's plastic dash. "I've never driven him anywhere. I've never even so much as sat in his Jaguar. I don't think he likes me. He clearly likes you."

Taylor scraped his muddy shoes together. "Me?"

"Yes, you," Kitner complained. "I'm his driver, and I'm driving you. Think about it." He ran a red light.

Taylor gripped the door handle with both hands.

Kitner slowed the car slightly. "You wait until Nichols sends you out on one of his wild goose chases. You spend two days in Clapham, going flat by flat, asking the same questions, only to be told to start again in Hammersmith. Nichols'll drive you right round the bend." He whipped the wheel, forcing the car to skid around a corner and throwing Taylor against the door. He saw the snow splashing in front of the car

Dawn broke, and they ignored it, swerving through increasingly busy traffic back to Blackfriar's Bridge.

Chapter 2

Sorenson

Bumping the ashtray, his hair in his face, Sorenson smelled dust and dried paint as he rolled onto his side. Bits of tobacco and ash fluttered under his bed where he had been sleeping. He peered into the blackness, struggling with the figure punching him in the stomach. Sharp rings on white fingers bruised him and robbed him of breath, frightening him.

"The money," the man said in sloppy, Brixton, vowel-crunching English. He grabbed Sorenson and shook him. "Where's it?"

He listened with displeasure, concluding: not an ordinary thief, or the man wouldn't have wakened him or dragged him from his bed. He felt the uneven planks of the floor of his Amsterdam studio as he was dropped, right shoulder hitting the wood.

He caught a glimpse of another man in a long coat pulling clothes from the dresser drawers, tossing garments left and right, and making a mess. The fluttering noise, followed by a loud intake of air though the nose, then a puffing out as if the mouth were sealed shut.

"Been some shortages," the Brixton man said, lifting Sorenson by his elbow, escorting him into the front room and dumping him into a winged-back chair. "Get it?"

"I sent it on," he choked out. "Not here." He pulled his T-shirt down, but it didn't cover much of his body, and he ached with the cold.

Three more crunching blows and bile spurted from Sorenson's stomach, mixing with blood, no air in his lungs and everything going dark around him.

Coming to, he made out the jewel settings of the heavy rings on the fingers of the more aggressive of his uninvited visitors.

He christened that man Mister-Rings, and the other Mute. The other wasn't invisible or hiding or timid, just not speaking.

Sorenson sniffed the acrylic paint and turpentine, enough to make his nose itch and eyes smart. He saw the shiny edge of paint cans and tubes amid the pile of cracked shelving, heard the squish and shuffle of feet trampling drop cloths, brushes, and paper. He must have really been out of it not to have heard all this.

These goofs were destroying his studio and thousands of dollars' worth of supplies. If they wanted money, why weren't they carting the lot off instead of trashing it?

A piece of shelving swung on one nail. He stared it, stuffed in his own chair, in his own flat. He couldn't move without pain—maybe a rib had been broken. Shivering, he shoved his hands under his armpits.

"Sent it on, did you?" Mister-Rings said, his heavy jacket rubbing the arm of the chair, his big body blocking out the dim light from the street-facing window. "Stupid toff." His thick fist glowed ivory close to Sorenson's eyes. "Well, it didn't get there."

"Didn't get there," Mute muttered into his ear, the voice rough, straining for projection.

More ripping of cloth and slashing of paper as his canvases became victims of knives and hammers. Whiffs of glue as a bowl overturned and crashed to the floor. Sorenson knew he had to take some action. He couldn't rush to the door—they were blocking it. He could inform them that the money had come here, that it had been attached to the backing of an English watercolor, that both the money and the painting had been sent onto Zurich, that, destroy what they liked, they would leave his studio empty-handed.

He might regret opening his big mouth, but details must be kept straight.

"You won't find anything," he said. "The money and the painting have been sent on. Days ago, to Zurich, as usual."

"Then what's this?" Mister-Rings held up a Nativity scene.

"That is a work I'm restoring." Sorenson rose, using the arms of the chair to push himself upright, and stretched out his hand. Whatever these lugs wanted, they had to understand that there was more at stake here than some idiotic collection of maybe-missing funds. Each work had a buyer, in fact, two buyers, one for the original and one for the copy. And payments went from London to Amsterdam to Zurich. These louts had no business interrupting that flow, no sense in shredding his work. "Please. It's worth a fortune. Let me finish it."

Mister-Rings slammed it against the window frame, splitting canvas and stretchers, a fragment of each remaining in Mister-Rings fist. He opened his hand and let the pieces fall to the floor.

Sorenson pointed, staggered with pain, aware he shouldn't anger them. "You idiot. I can't even salvage the frame." He braced himself against that same chair into which Mr. Rings had shoved him.

Mister-Rings grabbed him, shook him off-balance and punched him in the back, kidney-high. Sorenson crumbled, not wanting to see what they were doing, hating ignorant people, people who destroyed things for a living. He'd face the mess when they'd gone. Three weeks' work on that Nativity, removing the veneer, repairing the canvas, creating pastes and colors. Repaint it—he'd have to. Couldn't drop by your local '*everything*' shop and pick up pre-Renaissance religious artwork.

They were on him again, Mister-Rings poking him with a dirty finger. "You made us look. We looked. Now you look, and you find."

Mister-Rings dragged Sorenson by his hair.

He had never walked on his work before, never crunched his own canvases and frames with his bare feet. He stubbed his toe on the clawed foot of his chair. Swearing, he walked in a complete circle, over crushed paint tubes and cans, jars of adhesives, rollers, buckets, brushes, reference books, slide trays, all the way around his flat. The room had new dimensions with the piles of mess obscuring corners.

The wreck of his work startled him, inspired him, made him ache for his sketchpad and pencils. These piles signified "Thwarted Ambition," "Vanity." He imagined a new painting with allegorical elements: the drunken peasant, a waning moon, and evening star, wheat fields waving, volcanic mountains beneath a great cloud from which the blazing lightning sprang. He could never sell it as a restoration, but he could sell it. He needed to get these philistines out of here and get back to work.

"I found this." Mute held an open book close to Sorenson's eyes.

His stash and needles.

"Brett?" Sorenson had recognized the voice of Brett van den Dolder. But why was his voice so distorted? Sorenson stared at Brett's face, swollen, red, and seared. His lips seemed double their normal size. Maybe he'd been tear-gassed. Maybe that's why he couldn't speak. He must have been in that riot in Zurich. It'd been all over the news. "Why are you doing this? You know me. I never have money. Heather always managed it. You know that."

He fell against Brett, bumping his chin on the man's shoulder blade. They breathed the same gray breath. Alarm and agitation replaced Sorenson's surprise. "This isn't how we do things."

Brett pushed him off. "Things change, Sorenson."

"Hell, they do." Sorenson pushed back, touched Brett's super cool, smooth leather coat. "Call McIness. He'll tell you."

Sorenson pointed to where the phone should have been on a shelf that should have been. That name should have riveted Brett with fear, but he didn't flinch. Sorenson didn't understand this, so he tried a different tack, one designed to keep Brett talking. "What is this, Brett? Why are you trashing my work?"

Mister-Rings twisted Sorenson's left ear. "Pleasure."

"Knock it off." Sorenson hit out with both hands. Not that he posed much of a threat to men strong enough to stomp his work to bits. "Brett, tell him to knock it off. I don't have any money."

He remained close enough to Brett to see that he wasn't listening, that he wasn't interested in helping. He wanted Sorenson to suffer. He ground a palette, clicked a lighter, and held it low, revealing a mound of debris at his feet. "You're next."

Sorenson wanted out of his studio, out of Brett's

grasp. He estimated the distance to the door, the angle he'd need to twist to avoid both men, then to leap over the debris. Turning the handle might take more time than he had, given how close these guys were to him, but he'd have to chance it soon. He shoved Brett to get past him. Mr. Rings brought Sorenson down with a blow to the neck.

Splinters of palette scraped Sorenson's ankle and shin. He emitted grunts and growls of hatred and rage, rising up with both fists clenched.

Mister-Rings gripped Sorenson's elbow, thumb stabbing the arm above the bend, ending his escape attempt. Sorenson shook free and licked blood from his lip, scowling. "I paint, Brett. McIness sells. You distribute. You know, that's how it's been. Nothing's changed. Except that mess at your feet. That was a priceless Nativity scene. Due for pickup next week."

Sorenson fumbled, found the chair, and flopped into it. Breathing itself hurt. He wondered about how he'd sleep tonight with this much pain. He knew they'd take his stash, and he hadn't money to buy more.

"Got to do better than this, Sorenson," Brett said very slowly, swallowing after every word, his breath stale from cigarettes. "You were a thief in your cradle, Sorenson. You're a thief now. So, point us to it. Save yourself a broken nose."

Sorenson rubbed his eyes and shook his head in exasperation. "You broke everything in the place, man. Did you find any money? There isn't any money. Now, get out."

His work, his studio, crushed, slashed, gone. And it was two against one in the middle of the night in Amsterdam where no one was going to come to his aid. With all the parties he'd thrown in the past, his neighbors would think all the noise and screaming was some religious rite or a new erotic escapade. He needed a clear path to his door.

He sprang over the armrest. Mister-Rings slammed him back into the chair. Sorenson bent as Mister-Rings gave a rasping laugh. Brett's lighter flared, illuminating the lacy intersections of Sorenson's black spider web tattoo, the lines extending up and down his inner forearm.

"Clever," Mister-Rings said. "Draw it yourself?"

Brett tapped a closed switchblade against Sorenson's nose.

"Listen, Brett," Sorenson said, his voice breaking. "I'm not lying. There's no money here. None." He rocked forward and back, trying to loosen Mister-Rings's grip. "Get this guy off me."

Brett flicked the knife open, cold against the edge of Sorenson's cheekbone. "Where's Heather?" Brett sat on the armrest. "She ditched me in Zurich, the creepy little bitch. Where is she?"

Sorenson thought about correcting their opinion of Heather but concluded this was not the time for an argument over adjectives. That chain-smoking pixie was the smartest woman he'd ever met.

"Not here. Haven't seen her," Sorenson said, trying to jerk free from Mister-Rings's fingers. "What do you want her for?"

Like Sorenson didn't know, like Brett wouldn't want to stroke her small white body and plunge into it with the force of a bull. He remembered how Brett had made a play for her but that she had spurned him. It probably still burnt.

"What anyone would want a little bird like her for?" Mister-Rings said, the words rolling from his mouth, his body shaking.

Sorenson pushed sideways as Mister-Rings's grip loosened. But Mister-Rings moved more quickly than

Sorenson had expected, caught him by his T-shirt's collar, and twisted his neck backward, causing him to lose his footing and emit a moan. Brett's knife swiped Sorenson's face. He gripped his slashed cheek. Blood dripped through his fingers and ran down his arm.

"Brett, stop." Sorenson jerked to his knees. "Call McIness."

Brett shoved him to the floor. Sorenson wobbled to his feet, clawing over canvases, scrambled over the paint tubes and sketchbooks toward the door, toward the handle that would turn and get him out of this. A boot heel crushed the toes of his left foot, grinding the little bones.

"McIness is dead," Brett said. "You're on your own, Sorenson. No protection, no one to call on: alone."

Sorenson heard the window open, felt the cold rush of air.

They lifted him. Traffic noises rose from the street four floors down as he fell against the window frame. The December night air stung his cut face and mouth.

"No, listen." He grabbed the curtains, the casement, the ledge.

Chapter 3

Elias

Adjutant Beers waved back the onlookers as he opened the car door for the captain. Elias van den Dolder tucked the ends of his plaid woolen scarf into his coat, his gloved hands awkward. Sharp winds off the Amsterdam canals chilled him and slowed his progress. A cadet held an umbrella over him, the rain streaming down around them, the crowd craning, muttering. Their breath obscured their faces.

"We covered him, sir," Beers said. "Then we called you." He lifted the sheet with both hands, whipping more icy air into Elias's face.

Bending his knees carefully, the captain regarded the body lying flat on the boulevard. He touched the blood-soaked T-shirt, frozen to the man's chest, touched the white face, the long straight golden hair and the dark red stains. His American informant, someone's son, dead in a faraway place, blocking traffic and causing delays.

"Is it he? Sorenson?" Beers's voice rang in Elias's ear.

Elias nodded, his rimless glasses slipping down his nose. He stared at the legs of the pressing crowd. He hated their curiosity, wanted no more dawn calls on icy December mornings, wanted his retirement party now and not in three more months, wanted hot coffee and Beers to be the captain today.

"See this?" Beers rotated the body's right arm. He seemed so puffed and muscled in his bulletproof vest. "Quite something."

Elias touched the spider web tattoo, stitched so cleverly around the inside of the elbow. The collapsed veins looked black under the skin and had merged with the tattoo. "Takes up a good quarter of his arm. Any others?"

"Don't know," Beers said. "We haven't moved him."

Elias stared at the crushed head, the ice clinging to a slash on the face. He carefully rolled the face side to side. "He was alive for that. This man was tortured. Nobody heard any screams?"

"Taking statements now," Beers said, glaring at the young policeman with the umbrella. The bumping busybodies kept knocking the man side to side, causing the rain to splash down on Beers and Elias. "But the first we knew of it was a call from a motorist. Scared silly he was. Thought he'd run over him."

"I don't see any tire tracks, mud, exposed bone. Do you?" Elias reached a hand up to Beers.

Beers helped Elias stand. "No, sir."

"Send the driver on his way, if you haven't already," Elias said. "Mr. Sorenson will be with us for a while."

"Yes, sir." Beers gave the order via his radio, keeping an eye on Elias, who was staring at the cut on Sorenson's face.

"Cover him." Elias gripped Beers's arm, avoiding a fall on the slick street. "Tox-screen for heroin. Check for ante-mortem bruising."

Beers shouted at the crowd to move and snapped his fingers. Constables rushed forward and scooped up the body from the street.

"A look at his flat." Elias moved toward the brick building, cursed the long day before him, and all the necessary phone calls—to superiors, to Interpol, to Scotland Yard's art squad. He would have to call Olivar. He missed the talkative Yank, always the early bird with his computer printouts. Slim and small, a café-latte face and darker eyes, the bold, black moustache beneath which his lips often parted into a golden smile. How well he wore his slate-gray suits with their wide lapels and so many blue shirts. How different from his uniformed Beers.

Elias tottered toward the curb, Beers supporting him. He edged under the doorframe and pointed upstairs.

Beers shook rain from his black hair. "Open," Beers said and stamped the cold out of his feet. "Forced entry."

"Forced exit," Elias said, his lips barely moving.

They watched as the doors of the ambulance closed and the bystanders dispersed out of Blauwburg Square. Reporters rushed forward, constables intervening.

After a slow climb up stone stairs, Elias stepped inside, over broken frames, cracked jars of paint, ripped canvases: all the wreckage in the dead man's studio.

Beers nodded to those officers boxing up the mess. "Not much left."

"Anything whole? A note, a letter, a postcard?" Elias inched toward the open window. The wet curtains stuck to the frame. He peered out at the square, at the people crossing and entering shops. Trolleys spit their electronic noise as the rain sputtered and then stopped.

"Nothing we can decipher. Pieces only." Beers kept a step behind the senior officer, allowing him to view the scene without commentary.

Elias picked up a triangular piece of canvas, wet

from the rain. The Angel Gabriel, kneeling, halo and face shining, gold leaf, green-inked gown, and a white lily. He fingered an edge. "He was very good."

"Light-fingered, Interpol says. The Courtauld and The Tate both have works missing." Beers bagged the fragment. "San Francisco art squad also wanted Sorenson for theft."

"We've a list of what's missing from the Tate?" Elias slipped on a brush.

Beers caught him around the waist, righted a chair, and made him sit down. One of the investigators bought him coffee in a pink cup, the saucer chipped. Elias noticed that the other officers slowed in their work, turning or craning their necks in case he required more assistance.

"Not yet." Beers shrugged. "Sorenson knew, but he won't be telling anyone now. You'll have to go, take what evidence we have and present it to England's crown court. With our star witness dead, we've no case to take to our court."

"London." Elias spit out the word as if repulsed by it, by the nature of that brimming capital, alien peoples, and exclusive clubs. Himself years ago, a war refugee in his Dutch airman's jumpsuit, seeking a room to rent down un-sidewalked streets, stared at from doorways. This time, he'd come as a supplicant, bearing a slice of a scene, for the return of looted art. Sorenson had stolen more than one painting from the museums and galleries who hired him. He admitted to making copies of all the works he repaired, first as an employee of the Tate and then later as a freelance conservator. How many paintings Sorenson had worked on in Amsterdam was not yet known, that Beers would have to learn from these piles of frames and canvases. "I'll go by the night ferry. Sleep my way there." Elias drank and smiled. "You'll be in charge,

Beers. Don't let that idiot Rauda get in your way. God's own clown, that he is. Who hired him anyway?"

"You did, sir," Beers said.

Their everyday joke, not to be repeated nor laughed at in company.

Elias sat up, the cup jiggling in his two hands, pained, aware of the stench of blood, wood, glue, and unfamiliar oils. "Is he here?"

"Handling the reporters." Beers sipped his coffee. Bags of evidence were piled up around them.

Elias set his cup on the arm of the chair. "See any white paint?"

Beers narrowed his great blue eyes. "No, sir."

"Odd," Elias said. "Need white, don't you? For mixing colors?"

"Powder," Beers said, digging through the bags at their feet. He jerked toward the center of the room, staring. "Drugs."

He strode into the bedroom. Drawers slammed.

"Look for a wallet," Elias called, sinking against the worn fabric, the flattened cushion. "Look for bills folded like a triangle. They might still have some powder in them. Also, an address book, a client list."

Elias located a phone from under a bit of framing. He twirled the ripped cord with disappointment. He wanted to close the window and halt the terrible breeze chilling him. But there were too many people in the room, all busy with things he didn't want to think about.

He heard a whirring ring, muffled. A second phone, under a bed, maybe?

The click of a machine and a woman's voice, urgent and worried. Elias smiled as he recognized the voice of Sorenson's girlfriend, Heather Hiscocks. That little bird had returned and was calling from the train station. They could catch her there, and she would be another piece of evidence to take to London to set before Commander Nichols.

Chapter 4

Taylor

All one motion: answering the phone, standing up, looking at his watch, eleven-eleven a.m. Taylor flopped on his bed as he recognized Hines's voice. As if the day hadn't been long enough already, now he was wanted.

"Got a car?" Hines jabbed at him even at a distance, knowing what a sergeant could afford on what he earned. "Nichols wants you down here pronto. And before you ask, Five Filmer House, Filmer Road, Fulham. Write it down. I'm not repeating it."

"I work Southwark," Taylor said and squeezed under the bedclothes.

"Not today," Hines said, his words all shiny and barbed. "Commander calls, you go. Report to Sergeant Kitner."

Taylor stirred himself, cranky on his three hours sleep, and cowed. Hairs on the back of his neck tingled as he dressed, kicking drawers and closets closed.

Arriving in Filmer Road, he joined Kitner in his car.

He leaned toward the windscreen of Kitner's car. The parking brake poked his thigh. He allowed his head to sink, angry that he was out of bed to assist with an arrest. Surely a few constables could have been called up and stationed round the corner. They'd be eager to collar a murder suspect with the possibility of interviews with the press.

Still, Taylor kept his hand on the door handle, ready to move. Kitner seemed unusually relaxed, tie loosened, slouching, looking up and about as if a film were soon to start.

Maybe this was how detectives become working for Nichols. Maybe working for a commander was easy work, and everything said about Nichols was propaganda designed to keep the ranks from applying to his department.

"Letter box lists a 'Peter Jurg.'" Kitner pointed to an unshaven, blonde, young man leaving a three-story brick building. "And there he is, our suspect."

The thin man wrapped a black scarf around his neck, already encased in a black turtleneck jersey. Jurg coughed and grabbed at his throat with gloved hands, hurrying along the treeless pavement, heavily dressed, nothing but his rosy nose exposed to the rain and air. He avoided the puddles on Filmer Road.

"That puny, twitchy wanker?" Taylor frowned. "You think he strung up McIness? He couldn't lift a rabbit over his head."

"None of that," Kitner said. "You're here to observe."

Taylor stared, arms crossed, obeying.

Jurg stopped and coughed again, one hand over his mouth. He failed to look up and bumped into a large man in a black coat.

Neither man spoke, and neither moved. Then the big

man slapped a hand on Jurg's right shoulder. He stared at the gloved hand.

"That's Lake." Kitner's voice had the pitch of excitement. "You'll be working with him and his partner, Olivar. He's behind Lake, but you can't see him yet. Give it a minute, and you'll see Olivar swing about Lake and cuff Jurg."

Taylor sat up, perplexed, wondering why Kitner enjoyed this.

But just as Kitner predicted, Lake barred Jurg's way. He sidestepped, tried to flatten himself against the red brick wall that lined the rest of the street. His jaw muscles pulsed as if he were swallowing words. He waved his hands in the air as if in surrender.

Then Olivar emerged from behind Lake, caught one of Jurg's upraised hands, and wrenched it behind the man. He arched his back, struggled, as his other hand was pulled down and cuffed. Lake whispered something in Jurg's ear, frightening him.

"There's Olivar." Kitner pointed, whispering about Olivar's manicured nails, cropped hair, and Italian leather boots. "You see the little dance they do? Lake halts the suspect's progress and, before the man can object, up pops Olivar with the cuffs. Neat, quick, elegant, never a word out of either of them."

Taylor studied Olivar with his long camel coat, dark moustache, clapping his hands slowly. Taylor squirmed with unease. What did this mean to him? Why was he dragged out of bed to see this? He began to suspect that Kitner was jealous of Olivar and Lake, that he made fun of them because he never nabbed anyone but sat in his Mini waiting for his turn at glory.

Lake took Jurg by the arm and led him down the street.

Kitner laughed and rolled down the window a crack.

"Ever seen partners do it like that? Lake could take any man down with one hand, but he never does. He always gives the collar to Olivar. I'd never give the collar to someone else. You ever do that? Wait on your partner?"

Kitner turned on the car's ignition.

Taylor ignored Kitner and stared into the side mirror at the blurry maroon spires of an elementary school. He heard the crunch of gravel as he watched as a wide, wobbly wood gate rolled back revealing a warehouse, two police cars, and Henry Hines. He lounged against the boot of a silver Jaguar, smoking a cigarette under an umbrella. Opposite stood a brick bungalow with a small sign on the door, Office, Imports and Trading, Eugene Cohen, Proprietor.

Kitner jammed the Mini between the two panda cars. Taylor squeezed out of it, sidling. He elbowed the door closed.

He'd lost sight of Lake, Olivar, and Jurg. He didn't like the way Jurg was being treated: pushed and slammed about. Why was all this effort necessary? What could anyone fear from this Jurg? Why was he, Taylor, forced to witness this? If Nichols wanted Taylor to meet Lake and Olivar, why not use one of the rooms at Southwark Station instead of this street corner in Fulham? Was this why officers complained about working for Nichols, all this silly drama?

Then he saw Lake stuff Jurg into the nearest panda car.

As Taylor passed the vehicle, Jurg bumped the window glass with his chin, begging for release. The window fogged with his coughing and his crying.

Kitner had had an easier time getting out of his car. He'd immediately ducked under Hines's umbrella while Lake and Olivar climbed the warehouse stairs.

"He didn't kill McIness," Taylor said to Hines.

"'Course he didn't, couldn't have. A wee bairn like that hang a big man like McIness?" Hines crushed out his cigarette in the gravel. "But his arrest will get the brass off our backs. We'll look good for a week or two, until the next outrage." He gestured at Jurg. "This one really helps, a foreigner with an expired visa—"

Kitner interrupted. "Watch Lake with his master key."

Lake snapped a lock on the warehouse doors with huge bolt cutters he drew from a bag of tools at his feet. Olivar picked up two smaller containers, one shaped like a camera bag.

Lake slid the ten-foot doors open with one hand. The red burglar alarm clanged in objection. Taylor put his fingers in his ears as Olivar raced inside, found light switches, and turned them on. Lake replaced the bolt cutters in the bag and hefted it inside.

No one spoke until Olivar located the off button for the alarm.

Taylor wiped his feet as he entered the building. That set Kitner laughing, since sawdust littered the floor. Inside, four huge lights illuminated piles of boxes, barrels, packing materials, and tools. Clothing hung from rafters, which stretched deep into shadows and darkness. His ears still ringing, Taylor grew lightheaded, staring up at women's dresses, pirate costumes, togas, tabards, and tunics.

Kitner introduced Detective José Olivar and Detective Sergeant Michael Lake. Taylor shook each officer's hand, made friendly inquiries about their health, and waited for orders. He guessed they wanted his muscle, another Lake to break down doors.

Lake waved Taylor toward some crates. Together, they pried the front off of one, ripping at the slats with a crowbar. Wood splintered, dust flew. Lake tugged at the packing straw until an object emerged. He sliced through plastic wrap, brown paper, and foam rubber to reach a painting.

"Rubens." Lake laughed. "He'd had to have risen from the grave to have painted this. Look at those colors."

Olivar stared down at the canvas. "It's not what we're looking for, but what the hell." He took a Polaroid camera from his bag, clicked off a shot, and held the print in his hand while it dried.

"What is this place?" Taylor asked, staring at Lake's handiwork.

"Prop house," Olivar said. "We're supposed to believe that, but we don't." He stepped around Lake and took a photo of the back of the painting. "It's really a hideaway for stolen goods, at least that's what Nichols told us. So, we brought our tools, and he brought you. We'd like to know why?"

He handed Taylor the two Polaroids.

"I should like to know that as well." Taylor examined the photos, front and back, artwork reduced to a flat record. The two-dimensional account bewildered him. He handed them back to Olivar.

Olivar regarded the photos and then Taylor. "You don't know anything about art, do you?"

Taylor shook his head. "What was that charade out there?"

"You saw that, did you?" Olivar gave a satisfied smile. "Bit of theater for the neighbors, you know, big brother, long arm of the law, that sort of thing." He dusted off a table and placed the photographs side by side. "We want to know who's watching, so we give them something to see. Nothing big, just a little unusual."

"I see."

"Bet you do." Olivar held out his hand, palm flat.

Taylor slapped it, smiling.

"Stay with the big guy." Olivar pointed at Lake. "He'll keep you busy. And believe you me, with Nichols around, you want to be busy." He reached down and pulled a portfolio from the larger of his two bags.

A crunch of wood drew their attention to their left. Lake broke into another crate, leaving a trail of shavings and cracked slats. "Get the straw out, will you, Taylor?" he said. "I'll open this other."

Taylor stepped toward Lake, bent, and pulled heaps of straws from the broken box. Then he struggled with two small paintings, cushioned in plastic. He stacked them near the racks of costumes, enduring the prickle of the straw and its stale smell. He heard a crash and ducked instinctively before looking up.

Olivar waved from a jutting shelf. "It's okay. Nothing broken."

Then came fast steps on the stairs. The men looked up.

"Anything?" Nichols asked from the door, Hines at his side.

Taylor jerked to attention at the sound of Nichols's voice. Hines gave Taylor a wink then crossed the warehouse's threshold.

"The Dali? The Matisse?" Lake waited for Nichols's nod. "So far, nothing, sir." He unbuttoned his greatcoat. "The air waybills list this address, but we've found nothing like that in any of these crates. We had a look earlier at the receipts in the office. Nothing too informative."

"Sketchy as records go." Olivar pointed to a ripped label on an opened crate. "Household goods. That how it's listed on the waybill. Not even a note as to its size or shape. Who filled in this paperwork?"

"Big warehouse. You may yet find something," Nichols said. "Taylor, good morning. Please continue."

Taylor replied, but voices drowned him out. He

picked out the new bass sounds that were Olivar and Lake, distinguishing the growling tones that were Hines and Kitner. Taylor expected that they had already assigned him nicknames and spurious habits. He hoped Nichols wouldn't keep him long. Maybe if he proved useless, he'd be back in Southwark tomorrow, walking the strand while the moon rose and the skateboarders rattled down the walkways and ramps of the National Theatre.

"Catch that, Taylor?" Hines said. "You were miles away."

Kitner waved Taylor forward. "We're to bring our prisoner to the office, that tidy little building with the brick facade." He nodded toward the top of the car park. "Commander wants a word with him."

Taylor followed Olivar and Lake out of the warehouse, each wiping his hands, trailing straw. He watched as Hines and Kitner pulled Jurg from the back seat of the panda car.

"He's yours," Hines said as Taylor reached the car. He heard the office door slam and knew Olivar and Lake had gone inside.

"No more crying, eh?" Kitner said. "No one's hurting you."

Taylor laid one hand on Jurg's right shoulder and the other on Jurg's right elbow. He urged the unhappy man toward the office, telling him that it was warmer inside and there would be tea.

Jurg twisted, dragging his feet until Kitner and Taylor lost patience. They lifted him by his arms, jammed him into the office, and dropped him into a chair. Lake held the death photograph of William McIness to Jurg's face. Jurg kicked at Hines, refusing to look at the picture. Kitner yanked Jurg's hair, and he lifted his eyes to the portrait.

"Gene?" Jurg slipped from the chair, head first.

"Who?" Lake said and looked at the picture.

"What'd he call McIness?" Taylor asked as he sprang to catch the fainting Jurg. He sprawled on the office floor, hands still bound. Taylor righted him as Lake removed the cuffs.

"Not that gruesome a picture." Lake put Jurg back in the chair.

The office door opened and closed.

"Gene," a woman said. Cigarette smell as she spoke, the scent of citrus as she moved. "Eugene Cohen. It's whose office you're standing in. And why's the warehouse open? There's valuable stuff in there. It could all get nicked with the doors like that."

Taylor scanned the short velveteen black skirt, black coat, white face, dark red lipstick, and the dyed black hair. Black-heeled boots, widening from slim ankles to skinny knees. Boots, Taylor thought, nice legs, nice skirt—lose the black tights.

All the officers remained silent, even as Jurg stirred.

"Miss Suzanne Cooper?" Nichols said. "Glad you could join us."

"Mr. Cohen went missing three days ago," she said. "Why are you lot showing up today?" She put her small purse on the desk opposite and turned on a portable heater. "What's he doing in here?" She pointed at Jurg, who rose suddenly, aiming his body toward the door. Lake eased Jurg back into the chair. "He's not going to tell you anything, the little puffta."

"He's told us—confirmed, rather—that Eugene Cohen and William McIness are the same person." Nichols gestured to Lake to show the photograph of McIness to Cooper.

She stared at the image, her eyes beginning to blink rapidly. She turned away, dragged a chair from the corner and sat.

"We're hoping you might enlighten us further. Mr. McIness—Cohen, if you will—owns a townhouse in Putney, a flat in Mayfair, and a manse in Dover, and not one of these shows any sign that he resided there. Exactly where did he live?"

"Five Filmer House, Filmer Road, with him."

Jurg flinched at that remark and yanked his coat about him. Lake nudged him, and Jurg raised his hands as if expecting a blow. Taylor started forward, but Lake waved him off.

"Did he?" Nichols said, angling himself between Cooper and Jurg.

Taylor palmed his notebook and readied his pen. Even Olivar looked interested, scooting against the door, one hand on the knob.

"You see," Nichols continued, "it's rare that a banker has a second career as an import-exporter, even if retired, and Mr. Cohen was far from retirement. Rarer still that he kept no fixed address."

The upward tilt of her eyebrows confirmed to Taylor that Suzanne Cooper knew more of McIness-Cohen than she cared to.

"He owned property and lived where he lived." Cooper shrugged. "Where's the crime in that?" Then her voice softened. "He's dead, isn't he? I knew something had happened. He was like clockwork: through that door at haft eight every morning, briefcase in one hand, *Guardian* in the other. When he didn't arrive on Friday, I called you straight away. What did you do—nothing." Cooper crossed her legs as punctuation to her assessment of the situation.

Taylor thought her strong, fierce, a fit companion for a warrior. Nichols had only to keep her talking, and they'd have the whole mystery of McIness's death wrapped up in a bow.

"Yes, so you did," Nichols said. "Very conscientious of you. You're undoubtedly a very great help to Mr. Cohen. Perhaps you can be a help to us? Is there anything else you can tell us about Mr. Cohen? Regular appointments? Important clients? Someone you remember?"

"His business was all on the phone," she said. Her voice grew toneless, as if she were repeating a phrase for the twentieth time. "Almost no one came to see him." This she directed at Jurg, who'd hidden his head in Lake's greatcoat. She continued in a more excited tone. "Shipments came in and went out according to his schedule. I signed the receipts and filed the paperwork." She pointed to the cabinets.

The phone rang. They all waited while Cooper answered it and explained that Mr. Cohen was unavailable, but she could take a message.

She hung up the phone, with her head cocked, eyes glassy, and suspicious. "So, tell me, how'd he die?"

"Mr. Cohen was asphyxiated," Nichols said. "I've a few more questions for you." He dismissed Olivar and Lake with a wave. "Lock up the warehouse when you finish. Taylor, I'll need you to return in ten minutes or so." He tapped his watch, and Taylor stifled another yawn.

Chapter 5

Heather

Heather blamed Sorenson for her rotten trip from Zurich to Amsterdam, having to sleep standing up, straps of her rucksack digging into her shoulders, crouching every time she lit a cigarette. Even the smoking cars were smoke-free, so many families traveling with kids. The big louts in the hallways kept the windows wide open. The wind nearly blew her wig off. All to reach Sorenson, who wouldn't answer his phone.

"Pick up," Heather shouted into the phone. "It's Sunday, nine thirty-two a.m., and I'm ringing you from the train station. I wore the wig like you taught me, Sorenson. I smeared Noxzema under my eyes, so I'd look weird and ill, and nobody would talk to me. It's a Bosch painting down here: worn-out people sitting on their filthy bags in muddy corners, drinking like snakes from bent plastic bottles. Now some frog-lipped guy is banging on the booth. He's scaring the shit out of me. I will find you, Sorenson. I don't care what you're doing, or whom you're with."

She pushed the phone booth open. "What's your problem? Can't you wait your turn?" Cold air rushed through her clothes.

The guy grabbed her. "Sorenson's dead."

The fog of their breaths mingled. His voice made her angry. Who was he to interrupt her with lies? Heather rammed him with her pack. She ran from the station, bashing people out of her way, and swung herself into the nearest tram. She rode two stops, jumped off, and ran again. Then she fell, shaking, breathless, the heavy backpack overbalancing her. She saw bloody streaks in the green goo she was coughing up and cried into the needling rain.

Two Chinese musicians helped her up, and she clung to a mailbox in front of an open café. She tried to thank them, but she couldn't swallow, let alone form words for her voice would produce nothing except squeaks and whistles.

She felt watery, blue from the inside. She touched her forehead and finally accepted the fever she'd been denying all night, as her fuzzed brain wandered to a summer's day at the Zurichsee, a white tip of a wave and the splash on her face. She gave her head a shake as if that would reset her body's defenses and free her of illness. This wasn't how she had intended to return to Sorenson, not weak and unable to care for herself, lurching side to side down the city's streets.

She staggered to a seat in the café, embarrassed. With several hand gestures, she managed to order tea and drank, her eyes blinking, straining against the need for sleep. She must not sleep here, must find shelter, with a phone, so she could call Sorenson. He couldn't be dead. An unanswered phone call, some ugly guy's ravings, that was not proof. That was just to scare her, to keep her from Sorenson, but she wouldn't be deterred. If that guy at the train station was Brett van den Dolder, looking so peculiar, ruined, with brassy hair, and bulbous eyes, then that was reason enough to get to Sorenson's place straight away.

Her tea cooled, the honey congealed at the bottom. She looked at her pack on the floor, still there, not opened. No one had disturbed it or her. She thought again of Sorenson and Brett.

Her bulky pack beat her in the butt as she left the café and walked, yanking the wet straps to keep it centered. It was so big. It made her look like a ten-year-old runaway instead of the professor with advanced degrees in languages that she was.

Police tape encircled the Hotel Amster. Heather leaned heavily against the tram stop, watching officers conferring, measuring, photographing. She wanted a closer look but was too tired to move.

A hand clamped down on her shoulder, shaking her. She stared at the edge of a dark-brown leather coat, up at the red hair and eerie, dilated eyes. Brett van den Dolder: he'd found her again.

She stumbled, her pack wobbling. It broke the police tape as she fell, her shoulder slamming that of a constable. He grabbed for her and missed. Heather tasted mud and smelled the Vicks Vaporub she had smeared on her chest. The wig flew from her head and landed two feet away.

"You all right?" The policeman heaved her to her feet and then bent to look into her eyes.

She didn't respond though she understood, calculating how to get away from him.

"Bleeding," he said, his voice higher pitched than she expected.

She touched her face, her fingers red now with blood.

"Lucky the doctor's still here." He spoke into the radio clipped to his vest. His eyes were blue in a ruddy face, his hands wide and white.

She read his nametag, Rauda, as he hustled her indoors. Rauda seated her on the stairs. "Stay here."

A plump man in a gray raincoat stopped at the landing. "A live one, Rauda? You think I need new patients?"

Heather gripped the step as she coughed up more green ick. She breathed in gulps, trying to throw off her pack, the wide straps plastered to her jacket. Her wavy pale hair dripped with rain.

"Maybe not so alive," the doctor said. "Let me look at you."

Cold fingers stroked her throat, brow, and wrist. A colder stethoscope was slipped inside her bra. The doctor seemed a large and dangerous creature, his moustache glowing gold. He looked down her throat. "Wider." He patted her palm and then filled it with white packages. "Take two a day. Take them all. Go to bed."

Heather thanked him with repeated nods, stuffing the packets into her pockets, slipping into the backpack's straps, shouldering the pack.

"A little advice," he said, "Next time you run away from home, little girl, take a smaller pack."

At the open door, she surveyed the crowd before descending the steps, relieved that she located no red-haired man in a floor-length leather coat.

Waiting at the tram stop, she carefully examined the clothes and shoes of those around her, preparing herself to run if Brett appeared. She pulled her beret from an outside pouch of her pack and jammed it over her wet hair.

She knew the pack made her conspicuous but not for long. She knew of a women-only hostel. She hurried to get there, staying among crowds as much as possible. Out in the open, she was vulnerable.

Chapter 6

Taylor

Out of the Fulham Road office they came, and the streaming rain drove them as a unit into the warehouse. Taylor had thought to wait in the panda car for the commander's call, but Lake had a different idea: stack paintings, lug crates, and dig through stale straw for sculpture, odd bits of crockery, and paperwork. They needed evidence, and they had better find some before Nichols asked for it.

"You can't know," Lake said. "You haven't worked with Nichols before. If he says ten minutes, expect a half hour. He doesn't hurry."

So Taylor shut his mouth and worked amid the odd-sized shelves, the carpet-covered braces, the locked trunks and the hanging clothes. He hungered and thirsted in silence as all the dust swirled as the wind blew in and he searched.

Lake strode about the warehouse, his heavy, black coat flapping and stirring the shreds of packing material beneath tables. Occasionally, he stopped and banged on the wall with the crowbar, making notes in a black-bound book. The noise of this made Taylor look, but he didn't ask Lake what he looked for.

Lake grumbled in Irish. Taylor guessed the odd sounds were Irish.

Then Lake dropped the crowbar into his tool chest and pulled a chair up to the table at which Olivar shuffled Polaroids.

"It sounds solid enough." Lake pointed to the rafters. "But I'm sure there must be more to this place, at least one hidden compartment."

"Cohen, McIness, whatever we call him," Olivar didn't look up. "He's got three houses. Why hide anything here? Doesn't make sense. We're looking in the wrong place. That's got to be it."

Taylor saw his chance to rest. "Problem?" He liked to be of service, to learn new things, and his arms were getting tired.

"We got nothing," Olivar said, his black hair shiny from whatever gave it shape. He dated and initialed another photo, slipped it into a plastic sleeve inside a binder. His small hands were deft and brown. He wore a silver watch with large blue numbers. "We need evidence of fraud. We need at least one thing out of this whole mess that ties McIness and Cohen together as the same person. So far not a label, an invoice, a packing slip, or air waybill. And this knucklehead's beating on walls, looking for a secret treasure room." Olivar said this to the table, as he slapped the binder closed. "This was supposed to be open and shut, easy match, Cohen's export business to McIness's bank."

"You mean, the man at the bridge owned all this?" Taylor said.

Olivar nodded. "But McIness has been careful, doing business by phone, sending contracts by messengers, changing houses, and not making too many friends. Leading two very separate lives."

"You've got suspicions," Taylor said. "But you've no case."

"Exactly." Olivar kicked the leg of his chair. "Not like I can arrest a dead guy, but I'd like to close this case with at least one arrest."

"Make a nice, neat package for the magistrate." Lake picked up a pen, spun it, and dropped it. "It'd prove we've not been wasting Her Majesty's funds these two years."

Taylor wiped his hands, itchy from the straw. "Two years?" His cases lasted two, three days, one for the arrest, one or two for the paperwork and trial. Then, the case concluded, the file was dropped into a box, and off went the lot to the archives.

"Two years, and drawers full of notes and photographs," Olivar said. "You need piles of evidence to win a case about stolen art." He tapped the binder then jerked a shoulder toward Lake. "Which is why we keep this big lug about: somebody's got to haul it all into court."

Lake breathed on his bare hands, unruffled. "Irish slurs. He can't resist them. Pay no attention. I never do."

Taylor got it, went back to work, thinking about the bantamweight Olivar and the colossal Lake, how they became partners, what Nichols had them doing in this warehouse.

Taylor recalled the fable of the wren riding on a wing of an eagle. He branded Olivar and Lake with those tags.

Taylor suspected their association predated this case. They were old hands, skilled investigators, not the idle tricksters making quick arrests on street corners that Kitner would have had Taylor believe.

"So, I think we've finished with everything on the

floor," Olivar said. "Are those shelves next? Maybe we should haul some of this trash away."

"Over here, Taylor," Lake called. "Our leader has a plan, and it involves climbing. Bring that stool behind you, will you?"

Olivar climbed shelves, slunk between rows, and dragged packages to the front. He slid them to Taylor who handed them to Lake who stacked them on the floor. The routine halted when Olivar pushed to the edge an unusually large and odd-shaped, black chest with leather handles.

"You ready for this?" he asked. "Or should I break the lock and toss out whatever is inside?"

"It's evidence," Lake replied. "So, let's get it down in one piece. Just give us a minute."

Olivar jumped behind it, gave a thumbs up, and shoved the chest another inch.

Now Taylor craved a rest, but Lake waved him toward a strange forklift—no prongs, simply a platform that extended like a mirror might from a wall. They rolled it into the aisle. Lake flipped a switch, raised a handle, and watched as the wire-framed oddity reached the shelf where Olivar stood.

He slid the chest onto the forklift and then hopped on beside it. Lake lowered it to the ground, pried open the chest, releasing dust and dirt.

Taylor sniffed, sneezed, and examined the dirt streaking his uniform. Lake and Olivar shook speckles of sawdust from their hair, their coats, and their pants after removing heaps of cracked straw. They frowned at the contents: a small painting of skaters, blue and silver costumes, tambourines, and a circus poster with dogs on a balance board.

"Crap and fakes, a warehouse full." Olivar unbuttoned his overcoat, removed it, and flapped it several times before putting it back on. "Nichols said this was a genuine lead. Lead, my ass. Unless we're the ones being led, by the nose."

Taylor moved toward the dock for a chance to gulp fresher air. He rolled his shoulders, aware of kinks and strains that weren't there when he woke this morning. Street lamps glowed, and somehow it was late afternoon. His shift would be starting without him, and his mates would surely let him hear about it.

A car engine started, and Olivar sidled to the warehouse door. He elbowed Taylor as they watched Kitner back his Mini out to the street and park it against a curb. Lacking an umbrella, Kitner pulled his coat over his head and returned at a run. He yanked open the driver door of the panda car as Hines shoved Peter Jurg into the back seat. Kitner revved the engine and spun the police vehicle toward the street. Hines sat in the passenger seat, flicking ash out the window.

"Are they really going to take the poor man in?" Taylor asked.

"Looks like it," Olivar said. "It won't help us. We're stuck here inventorying this crap."

Taylor groaned as gravel and mud spattered Nichols's Jaguar.

Olivar said, "Nichols won't like that. No sirree."

The mess caused Taylor to look for a rag, something thick and soft, with which to clean the car.

"Won't like what?" Lake asked as he marched up. "Where are they off to?"

"Brixton, most likely," Olivar said, his hair losing its shape under the downpour. "Isn't that where all 'dangerous foreigners' go?"

Lake poked his square head out of the warehouse. "Those two won't drive that far. They'll dump him off somewhere local. Sod 'em. They're out of our hair. Let's be thankful for that."

Rain fell, drops large and slow, noisy and silver.

So how was this solving McIness's murder? Why was he, Taylor, losing sleep over crates of costumes and curios? It wouldn't get him a mention in the *Daily Mail*, or a visit to the Superintendent's office for a handshake, or even, more unlikely, a quick squeeze from Suzanne Cooper when he divulged the name of McIness's killer.

Still, Taylor labored on, as was his duty, aiding two investigators who needed him as much as a tiger needed a fork.

Later, Olivar called a break from the mindless work. Taylor sat on an upturned crate, rubbed his eyes, yawned, and rolled his shoulders, fighting fatigue. He thought of his mates at Southwark station, almost hearing their comings and goings through the new glass doors, the crackle of their plastic raincoats, and their complaints about understaffing and the frost in the air.

Then he found himself standing as he recognized that predictable hesitation of a Triumph motorbike downshifting. This was not the sound of a police vehicle, and its sound drew him to the warehouse door.

Taylor might not have any art training and couldn't spot a fake Gauguin from a real one, but set a motorcycle engine before him, and he could name every gear, plug, hose, or cylinder. He could take that Triumph apart and reassemble it before Olivar or Lake could spell Picasso.

The noise grew louder as the bike slid in the gravel and halted beside the remaining panda car in the carpark. The rider set the kickstand, his helmet under his arm. His dark hair was wetter than it should have been. Just out of the shower? Why the rush? Why had he covered his legs with rain pants but exposed that red-striped leather jacket to the violent weather?

Suzanne Cooper dashed to the rider's side with high, splashy steps. She wrapped her arms about the man's neck. They kissed, braced against the bike. Her black skirt rose and revealed the lace edge of her slip. Rain-soaked lingerie, silk tights, Taylor missed them now that they were not always drying on every surface of his washroom.

"You must live a dull life." Olivar flipped up the collar of his bright coat, his head bare. "If that gets you hard and stupid."

Teased again, Taylor's chin sank to his chest. He never had a stinging comeback, and he let Olivar have his laugh.

"What's the racket?" Lake brushed his hands and stared down at the two lovers by the motorbike. "Can't be."

"Don't doubt your eyes." Olivar nodded toward the biker. "Evan Nichols, and look who he knows."

"Christ Jesus," Lake said. "Now that can't be a coincidence."

Suzanne broke the kiss and pulled Evan by the arm. She smoothed her skirt across her bum with one hand, her hair sprinkled with rain.

Taylor waited for Olivar or Lake to order him back to work. Neither spoke or muttered. The young couple remained in their line of sight.

Nichols strolled toward them, turning up his collar, wincing at the tedious damp. His exchange with Evan and Suzanne was brief, with a few hand motions, a few up-turned heads. Then came a wave from Evan Nichols as Suzanne pushed him into the office.

Nichols climbed the stairs, not smiling. Nobody smiled at him.

"I've been on the phone." He gazed at the piles of broken slats, straw, paper, and artwork. "You'll have help shortly. Vans, lights, canteen." His hands remained in his pockets. "What have you found?"

"Chelsea Estates Gallery." Olivar pointed at the black binder, a pile of manila folders on the table, a stapled mound of invoices. "Lots of back and forth. Mismatched shipments, penciled-in items, under-valuations." With both hands, he displayed the stacked waybills. "But nothing from any museums' lists."

"Look for a safe." Nichols flipped through the bills. "We know he laundered money through his bank. There must be stocks, bonds, loan papers, and certificates of deposits. There have to be deposits."

Olivar pointed to the piles of paperwork. "He could have run the money through Chelsea Estates Gallery, bought stocks in the gallery."

Nichols lifted a waybill to his face. "Worth a visit?"

Lake set the crowbar down. "I'd say so, sir."

"Taylor," Nichols said, "will run me along to the gallery. I don't believe you'll get much out of Miss Cooper. But you can try. She has stopped crying."

Lake sat at the table. "We'll be gentle."

Olivar asked, "What about Evan? We question him?"

"He'll have to be told that his girlfriend is a person of interest in a murder inquiry." Nichols yanked at his sleeves, where the rain has collected. "Couldn't he find a girl in his college instead of in a pub?"

Olivar bobbed his head. "She could be the assistant she says she is. Keeps very neat files."

"And I'm Robin Hood," Nichols said.

Taylor gave himself another brushing, ready to meet-and-greet, ready to drive a Jaguar and to luxuriate in its leather seats.

He gazed at Evan's motorbike, shiny with rain. The sons of policemen, the sons of politicians, could never hide from their fathers' work. They were subject to the pressures of the profession from birth to death. Taylor's father had been a bricklayer. Nobody expected him to be one. Nobody approved of the police, but at least it wasn't the army.

"You want me to tell him or get a man onto her?" Olivar said. He brimmed with excitement. Taylor wondered why.

"On her," Nichols said, skin taut at the jaw line. He peered over the bottom rim of his glasses. "She may lead us to someone."

Olivar calmed, no grin. "You want a tap on her phone?"

"No." Nichols pursed his lips. "I want you two to have a word with Evan." Nichols cocked his head. "Describe your visits to the Courtauld and the Lamb. Make him see that he is being used. Separate him from her and worry him."

Taylor considered what his father's inference would do to Evan. Make him bitter? Hate his father? Quit college and join some cult in Morocco? Taylor would like to soften the blow for Evan, and yet Taylor didn't even know the young man. Who was Evan to Taylor? Merely a figure in the rain with a smart jacket and a shapely bird.

"Worry him," Lake repeated. "Make him understand his bird is a threat to his life?"

"To mine." Nichols shivered. "His mother's, his brother's. Suzanne Cooper has a reason for dating him, and it's not his good looks. And I'd rather his mother not hear of it, so don't get him into the news."

Taylor glanced at Lake, who looked at his feet. The three officers rocked on their heels, the downward click of their shoes, tapping out an irregular tattoo. Taylor tried to think of McIness's murderer and not of possible romantic calamities, the commander's strained family relations, and a probable comprised investigation.

Nichols handed Taylor the keys to the Jaguar. "No racing."

Evan hurried to them, face flushed, hands in his jacket's pockets. "Dad?" He moved close to the car, elbows in.

"Shouldn't you be in college?" Nichols stopped, the two almost toe to toe. Taylor studied father and son from his superior height. The father enclosed in his mac, the rain darkening his hair and reddening his ears. The son's shoulders rounded in a boxer's stance, waiting for bad news. Taylor admired Evan: his small face, blushing, exasperated, doe eyes shining, talking back to his father, this opportunity to impress Suzanne Cooper, and score another squeeze of that lovely bird.

"Her boss's been murdered." Evan pointed to Suzanne hovering at the office's threshold with her hand on the doorknob.

"Did she say by whom?" Nichols removed his glasses, wiped them.

"Of course, she didn't," Evan said. "She's got nothing to do with it."

Taylor looked over his shoulder. Olivar stood on the dock, coatless, resolute, chest forward, spine stretched, eyes straight ahead, as if the rain that drenched Taylor didn't touch him.

A minute passed as Evan and Nichols regarded each other.

"See you at home, Evan." Nichols pulled the door open and nodded to Taylor to get in. He welcomed the order and slid inside with only a slight bob to keep his head from hitting the doorframe.

He maneuvered the Jaguar into traffic, delighted by the engine's hum but unnerved by the brooding commander in the passenger seat. Taylor considered what kind of father Nichols made, how much time did he spend with Evan? Did they enjoy a Saturday match? Had they bent an elbow at their local? Did Nichols hand out school prizes and encourage Evan's friends to join the Yard?

Taylor wondered, if his father had intervened, would he have continued with his pursuit and marriage to Joan. Had he ever listened to his father? Given the slow traffic, the distance to Chelsea, and Nichols's silence, Taylor had time to consider this.

ɞɷɞ

Taylor's cheeks blazed, caught in Chelsea Estates Gallery's intense track lighting, conspicuous in his uniform among the sculptures on steel stands, the bright assemblages on walls, and the jeweled creations in cases arrayed in the cold gallery. He watched Nichols and the gallery owner, Emile Glanz, from the awkward depth of a beaten aluminum chair. Everything in the room was seemingly designed for small-arsed midgets.

He and Nichols had waited for the better part of an hour, the black-haired gallery worker, Vicky, insisting that the director would return at any minute from his luncheon engagement.

She brought them tea on a cart, placing a pewter tea service on the table before Nichols, then serving them digestive biscuits before retiring to a back room. Nichols gave her not so much as a raised eyebrow to her earnest apologies.

Now the hazel-eyed Glanz sat before them. He wore his gray-hair cropped close as if his head were more beautiful than his hair. He unbuttoned the two-button jacket of his gray silk suit. It rippled against his body as he crossed his legs, settling himself more carefully in a duplicate of the high-back chair in which Nichols sat.

Taylor thought Glanz a composite creature—not a sphinx, but more of an accident that a child might have created with color blocks: the body of a seal, the head of a sailor, and the feet of a kangaroo.

"Mr. Cohen handled deliveries," Glanz said as he added milk to his tea. He sipped, the edges of his contact lens visible only to Taylor.

"You never made the deliveries yourself?" Nichols asked.

He fingered a glossy catalogue on the glass table, which separated him from Glanz who tipped his head as he spoke, something glorious about his teeth in his pink mouth.

Taylor took notes, in spite of himself. Nichols might yet ask him for an opinion or an observation. If not, he would have a record of events with which to amaze his mates.

Nichols leaned on the table, turning pages of the catalog, head angled downward. "He handled the manufacturing as well?"

"Mr. Cohen bought paintings, posters, from theaters and film companies." Glanz refilled his cup. "He gave me a list and then brought me what I thought might sell. When they did sell, he delivered them. He had the trucks and the staff. It was a very convenient arrangement."

"You have a list of the works Mr. Cohen provided?" Nichols asked, his greatcoat draped over the back of the cherry-wood chair, his slender legs crossed.

Glanz smiled, but his lips seemed taut and white. "Monthly reckonings exist."

Nichols sat back in his chair, hands in his lap. "Would you provide these reckonings to my sergeant?"

Glanz rose. He gave a big sigh, which Taylor found unexpected and dramatic. "If your sergeant would return tomorrow."

Nichols stood. "Taylor will remain here. He'll assist you now."

Taylor bounded from the metal chair, setting it rocking with the abrupt motion. His body mimicked the tension between the two men. He didn't like this development, but he should have expected it. It couldn't be fatigue that dulled his senses. Something about Nichols stupefied him.

Glanz waved Taylor toward the rear of the gallery.

"One more thing, Herr Glanz," Nicholas asked. "Do you have a Swiss bank account?'

"Yes," Glanz replied. "Of course."

Nichols asked Taylor for the car keys. "I'll collect you," he told him. They all turned as the front door opened with a mad tingling of bells. Surprise rippled Nichols's face. "Hines, good afternoon."

Nichols made no introductions to Glanz. The director glared at this snub, at the insult, and the shower of rain on his gallery room floor from the men's clothing. Where did they park to get so wet? Taylor noted the time Hines and Kitner had been gone, two hours. Did they interrogate the prisoner or dump Peter Jurg in the nearest jail?

Taylor saw pleasure in Hines's eyes. Was he pleased by the mess he and Kitner had made in the gallery? Or did Hines come bearing news more worrisome?

Hines swaggered with triumph. He strode, resolute, the lord high executioner into his emperor's presence. "The prisoner, Jurg?"

Nichols gave Hines a bored raise of an eyebrow. "Yes?"

"Doctor says..." Hines lowered his voice and watched Nichols's deliberate nod. "Peter Jurg may have the flu, but he's got tracks up both his arms and in the neck. 'A right nasty habit' was the doctor's view."

"Candidate for the infirmary," Kitner said, one big grin.

Nichols urged Taylor with a get-on-with-it wave.

Taylor took slow, small steps, listening. Hines and Kitner interested him. They'd made use of Jurg. Would they make use of him? How could he stop them?

"We've had another word with the solicitor, Hutchinson." Hines smiled, shoulders back in a wide, strong stance. "He admitted to knowing Eugene Cohen, but not knowing him as William McIness."

Kitner glowed with pride. For this one moment, he stood entirely convinced of Nichols's appreciation. But he kept his focus on Glanz who had paused at the back of the gallery, buttoned his soft jacket, his hairless fingers almost twirling the buttons into place.

Taylor stood behind Glanz, catching only vowel sounds but not the words Hines continued to exchange with Nichols. Glanz craned his neck as well but grew irritated as Hines drew closer to Nichols who nodded in response.

Finally, Glanz led Taylor through a beige door. His mind buzzed with all the scenes he'd witnessed this day: the arrest of Peter Jurg by Lake and Olivar, the arrival of Suzanne Cooper, and then Evan Nichols on his bike, the drafty warehouse chock full of paintings and props, and now this gallery all silver and glass, and Glanz elegant and strange in his alluring suit and fierce hair style.

Glanz indicated a back room, olive in color, with a dozen cabinets to match. The tall cabinets each had six drawers, and Taylor estimated how many hundreds of files each would contain. Above the cabinets hung harsh, florescent lights. They crackled and conferred on the furniture a sanitized glow.

"The cabinets are not locked," Glanz said and left.

Taylor faced the staggering task, no help, no chair,

and no knowing the consequences of not finding evidence of complicity in murder.

He found an A6 pad and ruled in columns for names and dates, while he wondered if he still had a post at Southwark.

He begged to use the phone and learned from the officer on duty at Southwark that he, Taylor, had been seconded for the duration of the investigation.

"And aren't your ears burning, you filthy sod? And who-the-hell do you know at Scotland Yard, you skivvy prat?"

His insides kicked and his feet refused to move—for *duration* had the connotation of punishment. There'd be no early release from Nichols, no quick return to Taylor's regular slog, not for him, and not in the foreseeable future.

Chapter 7

Elias

Still in Sorenson's damaged studio, Elias listened for Beers's return from Sorenson's bedroom, shifting in the big chair as an officer finished photographing the street-side casement and closed that cursed window.

Elias thought about heat, heating bills, the room's volume, the crime investigation team, and the unlabeled piles of evidence at his feet. Such a mess, such a waste, and the icy place made his bones ache.

The style of this wreckage interested him. This was such a thorough a job, the wood frames in splinters, the canvas in strips, and the paint tubes stomped. Not thieves, they would not have taken so much time, nor destroyed saleable property. Not drug dealers, they would have pawned the paintings. Assassins, though, would go for the artist and this had all the marks of revenge; your work, then you.

"Here, sir." Beers presented him with a leather portfolio, tied with faded strings. "Inside the mattress.

Sorenson sliced under the piping. Stuffed this in from the bottom. Very clever."

Beers pulled a chair flush with his armrest, their knees forming a table upon which Elias opened the large folder, revealing numerous drawings, sketches of heads, angel wings, draperies, and female nudes.

"Her again." Beers held up a pencil drawing and a charcoal sketch as proof. "Why not? She's beautiful."

Other officers stopped and craned their necks.

"Look for a name," Elias said, smiling—grinning, really.

Beers flipped the first paper, scanned it as a heavy clumping reached the door. "Rauda, what kept you?" he asked.

The breathless officer stopped in the doorway and motioned with his hands. "Ran. Stairs."

Beers waved him over, placed the drawings in an open folder, and fetched Rauda a chair. The young officer stared at the pictures, his eyes narrowing, and his mouth moving. "Seen her," he said. "Downstairs."

"Fetch her up," Elias urged. "Now."

Rauda pushed himself out of the chair and then lumbered out of the room.

Beers shook his head, watching him leave.

Elias flipped through the pictures of Sorenson's girl a second time, the wide mouth, dangling cigarette, cropped hair, rosy touches to her cheeks, knees, and hips. "Lovely girl."

He'd had a wife, not a girl, a beautiful wife with yellow hair. Dead, leukemia. Alise wasted away. Their boy, Brett, named for her great uncle, grew like a weed, with her soft eyes and the van den Dolder nose.

Chagrined, Rauda returned without the girl but explained that she was ill and the ME had given her antibiotics. Elias waved Rauda's excuses away. If she were ill, she wouldn't get far. They'd find her in a day or two.

In his office after lunch, Elias stared at the clean metal desk that had so recently been heaped with files and legal pads. Olivar had sat there, working side by side with Beers, documenting and often locating stolen art, with his Polaroid camera, auction catalogs, and notebooks.

Elias could still hear Olivar, his American accent, his habit of clicking his tongue in disappointment, the thrumming deliberation of his fingers, his elbowing will, and caustic spin of sorrow. Young Olivar, Art Squad of San Francisco, seconded now to the Metropolitan police.

Elias spun a pencil on the surface of his desk and fretted about the case the American had been making. He opened a blue file and reread the fax: *McIness dead. Bring Sorenson.*

He knew he must call Olivar, tell him about Sorenson, about the hitch in the case, and the damaged artwork. How would he, Elias, explain the loss of evidence and the loss of his critical witness? Olivar would be disappointed. He needed Sorenson alive, needed the artist to document his activities, trips, and associates. Olivar needed resolution, success, and a letter of praise for a job well done.

He would have no wish to view the crushed body. Not squeamish but easily discouraged, Olivar had a sunset nature, a mind bright with the last light of the day, the last light with which to see things clearly. In his absence, Elias felt a deep and confining darkness.

He shifted the blue folder and stared at the Polaroid of the Orphans of Amsterdam.

The first work identified by Olivar as Sorenson's, his little gold S in the right corner, not there in the original.

Olivar had found the identifier using X-ray.

"Sorenson was very good," Elias said out loud before

picking up the handset and began to dial, country code, city code, and lastly the local number.

Beers entered with the coffee tray, set it on his own desk. He shielded the pot as he poured. Elias watched Beers's elbows as they bent. He smelled the coffee, heard the stirring motions, held the cup in one hand, and tasted the sugar and cream, as he liked it.

"Olivar," the known voice on the phone, so flat and so unwelcoming.

"Joe?" Elias asked. Olivar told him to call him Joe. "I received your fax. Bad news. Sorenson." He closed his eyes. "He is here, in our morgue. Dead." This last word slipped out. It was redundant.

"No," Olivar said. A scraping sound of a chair on tile.

"Fell to his death last night," Elias stated, smoothing the unease out of his voice. "Terrible mess." He pulled the phone away from his ear as Beers leaned in.

"Fell?" Olivar's voice was loud. Elias held the receiver flat in his hand "What do you mean 'fell'?"

"Out of his window." Elias mellowed his voice. "To the ground."

"No," Olivar said again, softer. "You took pictures of the crowd?"

Elias and Beers frowned at the urgency in Olivar's voice. They clunked their cups down simultaneously, eyes fixed on each other.

The crowd they had kept at bay, pushing the people back to the curbs. Elias and Beers had sheltered under an umbrella, the rain obscuring even the pants' legs of the onlookers.

"Elias," Olivar said. "Tell me you took pictures of the crowd."

Elias looked at the stilling liquid in his cup. What could he remember? He struggled to recall the scene: the circling tram, thickening crowd, the rattle of voices, and the body bleached by rain. He felt his jaw slacken as perplexity contracted his lungs.

"No," he said, his voice cracking. "No pictures. I'm sorry."

He didn't bother with excuses. He himself could make up for the loss, if he went to England, if he testified.

Beers slumped in his chair as Elias hung up the phone. "The murderer could have been there," Beers said. "All that rain. I didn't think to take pictures of the crowd."

Elias nodded, his focus shifting inward. His son, Brett, with his love of knives, his American switchblade, stainless steel. That precise cut on Sorenson's cheek was more than a wound, more like a signature, like a master's final stroke.

"Turkey." Beers slapped his desk. "We traced Brett to Turkey." He paced back and forth between the two desks.

"That was months ago," Elias said. "Brett could've returned. You'll have to assign someone to watch his old haunts. We can't allow him to kill again."

"Sorenson's girl?" Beers asked, halting, facing Elias.

"Yes." Elias stared down at his half-drunk coffee. "She's next." He cleared his throat. "We'd had better find her before he does."

Chapter 8

Heather

In the hostel's garden, Heather woke curled against a tree, stiff and cold. She was unaware of how much time had passed. She'd broken her own rule: she hadn't remained hidden. She had fallen asleep outside and exposed herself to danger. She covered her mouth with both hands and rocked to stave off the coughing. Then she cursed herself for falling asleep, risking discovery. She should have smoked in her room even if it was forbidden.

Lights illuminated the hostel's second floor. Doors banged. Women shouted as a man bounded out the back door, hit the paved walkway, and dashed toward the gate in the rear of the garden. A lean man, agile, familiar, no hat, bare hands. He hadn't seen her, pressed as she lay in the crook of a willow, her cigarette butt in the thickened ice at her feet.

Two girls in pajamas rushed at the man, hurling rocks or mud.

Yes, girls, Heather thought, *drive the predator from*

*the nest. Give me the time to slip through my window and
tuck myself into bed.*

Someone turned on the outdoor lights, and Heather
pressed her body to the icy ground. Pain jabbed through
her breast. She pulled her knees to her chest, beating
them with her fists and deflecting her attention.

She wanted to be safe, but anywhere Brett could find
her was not safe, not here, not Zurich. She'd seen him in
Zurich: a still figure in that riot at the student center, the
Rote Fabrik. Brett had stood in the street, not running like
the students, not charging like the police. He'd stared at
her as tear gas spun from canisters, misted the street, and
a student with a bandana over his mouth hurled a rubbish
bin through a jeweler's window. Glass sprayed into air
already foul and thick. Brett had not moved, except to trip
a policeman.

Brett had frightened her more than the riot. He meant
harm, that was clear. She had escaped through the center's back door, pushing, fighting, running to the
Bahnhof, and boarding the first train going east.

෴

She grabbed the tree trunk and clawed herself upright. Empty now, the yard stretched dark and wide. She
reached her window with effort, climbed inside, and sat
on the bottom bunk, thankful her bad cough had gotten
her a single staff room with a toilet and washbasin.

She should've gone to Morocco, donned native
dress, and never been seen again instead of risking this
visit to Sorenson. But deposits had been short. Somebody
was skimming. She hoped it wasn't Sorenson, her beloved, foolish Sorenson, now dead, and Brett in town
again.

She rolled onto the bed, wished for a horse, a plane,

a magic carpet to whisk her away to Le Havre, Le Haye, London. She'd have to travel, but she couldn't stay awake long enough to even smoke a cigarette. Sorenson was dead, so who else could help her? Someone with a car, with money, with a reason to flee as strong as hers. She thought hard and then that one perfect name flashed into her head.

Willem Jurg, he'd help. He knew everybody, and he fancied her once. More than once, he offered her drinks at his club. He'd whispered in her ear Dutch endearments she half-understood. He had always wanted her to leave Sorenson, especially after Sorenson became friends with Brett. She wanted to leave then, too, but she had never admitted it.

She thought of Sorenson, the hand-rolled cigarettes he smoked, the ugly shoes he wore no matter what she suggested, and the pointed lips he curled forward when deep in thought. How many piles of sketches littered their bedroom floor, sketches of her in her nakedness? And Sorenson's nakedness beside her, his hairless chest that he'd hated and that she'd liked to kiss and stroke. Of course, there were all his bad jokes, the good smokes, and all the fine food. How incompatible, an Englishwoman and a Yank. If she could believe that, would it make his death easier for her?

She gripped the blanket to her chest and cried, slowly stilling her body but filling her mind with new ideas. She pictured again the running figure, Brett, escaping, not risking an end to his freedom. She knew what would harm him: captivity. That was what would kill Brett van den Dolder: a cell, a timetable, someone else in charge of his moves. There would be her revenge, a life for a life.

She must get out of Amsterdam, go to England, to her home where she knew the laws and knew how to manipulate them to her advantage. Yet she must act as if she was fleeing and make Brett follow. He must never realize her plan and his danger. She needed help, lots of it, as she was so ill.

She fell asleep, having formed a plan that would require Willem's help.

Chapter 9

Taylor

Called out to Nichols's home in Hampstead on a Saturday, told to wear civilian garb, jeans and trainers, and to lock his bike in their garage, Taylor had obeyed even though he couldn't relax in Nichols's sitting room with its yellow chintz curtains, matching striped pillows, and that smooth table too low for anything except for cracking a shin. He noticed all the fragile things—small table lamps, thin-legged side tables, colored glass vases, silver frames, and rugs with fringes. He couldn't live among them and wondered how Nichols did, though he was a much smaller man.

In front of Taylor sat Nichols's bony-faced second son, Parry, in a navy-blue striped dressing gown and pajamas. Parry had spread an encyclopedia of motorcycles upon the table. He seemed inured to the chilliness of the sitting room with its tiny grated gas fire.

Fully dressed, the cuffs of his black jersey turned back, Evan lounged opposite in a fat, leather chair. Taylor judged that Evan had very recently arrived home rather than having risen early on a weekend morning. The smell of cigarettes clung to his clothes and hair, another indicator that he had but lately exited a club.

Taylor listened attentively, on the edge of his seat, not because the high-backed chair wasn't big enough, but because he wanted just that extra inch to look down upon the color pictures.

"There are only six photos of BMWs," Parry said. "None of the newer models."

"Never had a new one," Taylor said.

Evan crossed his legs, his black leather shoes unmuddied and narrowed-heeled. "Neither have I."

Taylor understood that Evan had seen all the pictures in the volume, but he didn't spoil Parry's fun. Taylor almost gave out a great sigh, expecting that he would never be friends with Nichols's sons, that this strange meeting was a holiday for all of them, an early Christmas, not an event ever to be repeated.

He watched Parry read out statistics: engine size, gas tank volume, RPMs, and dates of manufacture. Parry didn't dwell on color schemes or accessories. He pointed to the contours of the bikes, the height of the tires, the width of the handles, and the races won. Taylor accepted every word as he had accepted the tea and toast Mrs. Nichols had prepared for him earlier in the over-bright kitchen.

It all made Taylor smile. Parry was a true enthusiast, Taylor was merely a devotee of speed and empty roads.

Evan drummed on his jawbone as if he would be doing something else, perhaps holding a cigarette to his lips. But this was a smoke-free place without, ashtrays, lighters, or any tin waste bins.

Taylor pointed to a bike that he'd own if ever he came into money. Parry disagreed and informed him that what he should buy was a 1951 Triumph, completely

British, and he could fix it with simple tools.

"In my spare time?" Taylor said. "I think I'll have some in 1999."

That stirred Evan. He nodded vigorously. "You and me both."

Parry shuffled forward, held the picture book up for Taylor to take. He set it on his knees, and this pleased Parry.

Nichols called his sons by name, but it was Taylor, shifting his eyes to the doorway, who started up, almost dropping the book.

Shadowed by the hall light, Nichols seemed slighter than his sons. He slipped his hands into the pockets of his mac, his scarf tucked close under his chin. He told the boys to mind their mother.

Taylor made his goodbyes, returning Parry's book, shaking hands, and expressing a genuine hope to meet again. Evan extended his hand, and Taylor took it with a slight incline of his body.

Mrs. Nichols stood by the front door, observant, in a fisherman's sweater and corduroy trousers. She touched Taylor on the elbow and smiled at him as he looked down at her. She stood barely an inch or two taller than her eleven-year old son, Parry. But she didn't have a boyish figure. Her hips had widened, and her breasts had rounded. She'd told him to call her "Jean," but he stuck to Mrs. Nichols.

"You will dine with us?" she inquired.

"We'll be back very late," Nichols said before Taylor could answer.

He thanked her, confounded by her kindness as she handed him his coat. He searched for the verbs of civility and concern, phrases of delight, but he flubbed it. His mind felt cold with sleep deprivation. Nichols led him to the Jaguar, now at the curb, and signed to him that it was unlocked and he should settle himself in.

The rain slashed against the windscreen as Nichols eased the car into traffic. He talked about his family, his wife, Evan's future, and Parry's mind. Taylor treated the news as gossip and forgot it.

Nichols glanced at him. "Your family, Taylor?"

"Parents and two sisters, Amy and Anne," Taylor said, cushioned in the fine leather seat. As the heat rose up his legs, he shifted to allow the air to warm to pass without singeing his clothes. He hadn't considered the pleasures of luxury before this. Cozy and cushioned never defined his driving experiences. Was he changing his mind? Ready to give up the bike? No, just a passing thought on a rainy day.

"Twins?" Nichols's voice rose a notch.

"Double trouble," Taylor said, amused. "Used to gang up on me until I was big enough to hip-chuck them. Dad put a stop to that."

"Wife?" Nichols turned those big eyes on him.

"She tired of the copper's life." Taylor blushed, not liking this, the image of his ex-wife, Joan, filling his mind. "Too much ironing, mending torn shirts, stopping bloody noses."

"Your captain says you've been in some scrapes."

"Take down the biggest guy first," Taylor said. "The rest go quietly. That's my motto." He closed his mouth, having made his point.

"David and Goliath." Nichols turned on the radio: news broadcast of weather, flooding, and road closures. "We're meeting Captain van den Dolder. He shouldn't have much luggage but take it from him." He stared at the road. "It's your day off, so I thank you for accompanying me. But, if anyone asks, you never went to Harwich. Evan accompanied me. You understand?"

"I slept in." Taylor rubbed his eyes, stifled another yawn.

Nichols eased the clutch out as the light flashed green. "Your super said you didn't take any holidays last year."

Taylor didn't want to discuss his finances or his love life or his unease of traveling alone. "No, sir."

"I recommend you do."

Nichols accelerated toward the motorway. He turned the wipes to high. The blades sloshed the rain into flying strips. "How ever do you work nights?"

"I sleep during the day, sir." Taylor yawned and his eyes closed against his will. He slipped into sleep with his head against the window glass. He dreamed of Suzanne Cooper in her short, swaying skirt and of his lips kissing the narrow inlet of her palm as her lips brushed his cheek tenderly.

Chapter 10

Elias

Knees pressed together, Elias perched on a bench under an awning on the top deck of the Dutch ferry. Shivering in his raincoat, hat, and gloves, he kept the black portfolio on his lap and his valise at his feet. He listened to the passengers bumping their way down the gangplank: scrapes of shoes, squeaks of luggage wheels, voices popping, echoing off ships, cranes, and containers on the Harwich dock.

He determined to be last. He had thoughts to settle. Sorenson had been his trump card, his in-road into the trafficking of art, his credentialed artist and expert witness. Sorenson, the skilled forger with fakes in the greatest museums in the world, knew the names and dates of the stolen works. In many cases, he had sketches of the works.

Elias had waited to arrest Sorenson until his girl, his muse, Heather Hiscocks, had returned to Amsterdam. Elias needed them both to prosecute the fraud case and reclaim the stolen art.

But Sorenson got a different deal: death in an Amsterdam square, a cracked skull, leaving his woman on the run, seen but not caught.

Cagey, that one, Elias thought. *Let her roam. She will come to me. She'd have to come to me. Brett will drive her to me.*

A touch on his elbow, his name called, he didn't open his eyes. He put a hand on the hand taking his valise. He heard the brush of woolen trousers as the person stepped back. Elias looked at the uniformed constable and his partner. No one smiled. Miserable country.

They escorted him through a continuum of levels, rooms, and doors. One held him by his elbow, the other walked behind. No visit to customs, no registry card, and no stamp in his passport. Certainly, there were no comments about the wet December morning, rough crossing, or the lateness of the ship.

Nichols waved from the window of his Jaguar, engine humming: a meeting of old friends and a bigheaded man in the passenger seat.

Elias rode in the back, his valise beside him. "I would like a coffee," he said, all lethargy, old.

"You'll get a whole breakfast," Nichols said. "I owe it to you and to Sergeant Taylor here. I've dragged him from pillar to post this week."

Nichols slowed the car as they reached a guarded exit.

Elias knew the words the men would exchange and didn't listen.

Chapter 11

Heather

Startled from sleep by voices in the hallway, she remembered her location: women's hostel, Amsterdam, Sorenson dead, and Dutch police in the square beneath his studio. She felt hunger and thirst as her fever had retreated. She thanked that strange doctor who pressed those antibiotics into her palm.

She washed her face and chest in the little sink. She dressed warmly—jeans, jersey, coat, socks, and shoes. She stuffed her passport and wallet into her pants' pocket. Wrapping her red paisley scarf tight around her neck, she admired herself in the mirror before she slipped out the hostel's window, not daring to leave by the front door.

She had to get to Willem quick, then out of the city, and across the Channel. She pulled her navy cap down over her ears, laughed at her escapade, though the action of her chest made her sob.

Easing down an alley in the red-light district, she located Willem's club, locked and bolted shut. She went round the back and, using her Swiss army knife, pried open one of the basement windows. Squeezing inside, she crawled over casks and boxes then rested, her eyes adjusting to the darkness. Gripping the railing as she climbed, she called Willem's name loudly as she pushed into the kitchen. She found chairs piled on the two Formica tables, the air stale from stubs of cigarettes in cut coke cans, linoleum remnants under the baseboard and the cooker. The larder door creaked, and a big-eyed man peeked out.

"Heather? What are you doing here? How did you get in? Don't tell me." Willem kissed her. "You look like death. Sit down." He pulled down a chair, his long blond hair falling into his eyes.

Heather feared the chair wouldn't hold her weight, but she sat in it.

"I'll put the kettle on," he said. "Then you can tell me why you're here. If it's another fight with Sorenson, I can't help you."

She shifted her weight, heard the chair creak. "Club not open?"

Willem cleaned a teapot as the water heated. "Police raided us last week, looking for drugs. Drugs in Amsterdam, what a shock. And a teenage girl, American. Shipped her home straight away." He tore shreds of invisible paper. "Rip went our permit. Club gone. And you? How's Sorenson? Haven't seen him lately."

"Dead." Heather's voice quavered. She wanted to take her words back, wanted them not to be true, hoped for a different way to reach Willem, to be soft and fine, and make everything seem his idea.

Willem touched a thick scar behind his left ear. His knees bent, ready to jump or run. He stared at the unshuttered windows. His brown eyes widened. He reeled. "Killed?" he cried. "No."

She saw him clutch at the scar, perhaps willing it to

vanish, to be an innocuous scratch, and not a testament to an attempted murder. She spoke with difficulty, her throat so sore it hurt her to breathe. Dizzy with fever, she pushed herself from the chair.

"I've seen Brett," she said. "In Zurich and here. I didn't recognize him at first, dressed so oddly. Leather coat to his ankles and dyed red hair, puffy face. But it was him. He's here."

Willem collapsed at the news. "Thought he'd gone to Turkey."

Heather slipped into his arms and shook him, her eyes hard.

He buried his head in her lap. "I know Sorenson thought Brett such fun, but Sorenson never owed him anything."

Heather leaned to keep his head from hitting the floor. She hushed him with a lullaby. The little song she sang ended in coughing and tears. She considered the frightened man, the under-heated room, the reason to go on with it all, to flee and hide, and how she herself wound up quivering and sobbing on a bare floor. She blamed Sorenson, but that didn't get her anywhere. She knew what he was like the first time he bummed a cigarette on the platform of Earl's Court Station, winking, connecting the dots on the underground map into faces of dogs and ducks. How he magic-markered mosaics on the edges of doorways.

With Brett in the old Fulham flat, unpacking drugs, Sorenson in his white clothes prying open carved frames with screwdrivers and steel wedges, wrenching out the baggies from the hollowed-out wood. The two men stacked neat piles of kilos in a crate by the sofa. Sorenson whistled while he re-glued edges and brushed lacquer until the stench drove them all to the café across the street.

With Sorenson in the dark sanctuary of the Nieuwe

Kerk where he loved the morning light, kissing, his hands up her shirt. That was a better memory. She dwelt on it for a moment before continuing.

"Brett came after me. He must have followed me from Sorenson's place. Some girls chased him from the hostel." She stroked Willem's coarse hair and used her hat to dry his face. "Pelted him with mud." She smirked. "He didn't find me having a smoke under a willow."

"He'll find you," Willem said. "He'll cut you. He likes it. You've got to go. I sent Peter away, to London, so van den Dolder couldn't get him."

Willem's body grew heavy in Heather's arms. His breathing slowed, and he stretched out his thin legs. She watched as he blinked away his tears.

"It's cold," Heather said. "Ever think of putting down a rug?"

"Don't usually crouch on my kitchen floor," he said.

She heard steam shoot from the kettle. "Never seen you cry."

Willem stood and turned off the burner. "Everybody cries. You're as bony as a broomstick. Are you on that 'all-air' diet?' You know, and they all go bare, and they live on the air."

Heather poked him in the stomach. "Look who's talking."

His zippered sweater sagged. "Now you really must go." He spooned tea into the pot. "I won't be insulted in my own place." He poured the heated water over the tealeaves, stoppered the pot, carrying it and a pair of lavender serviettes to the table.

Sitting at the table, Heather yanked her cap over her ears, shivering, counting the hanging pots and pans on the opposite wall, wanting to paint the walls with bold stripes, wondering how Willem could live here without decorating or putting up some posters.

Willem poured tea into blue mugs.

She took a mug in both hands. "I have to get out of the city."

"I guessed that when you didn't use the door," Willem said.

They drank. The hot tea made their lips red, a swelling vapor of chamomile rose between them.

"What day is it?" Heather asked. "I've been out of it."

"Wednesday," Willem said. "You'll need more clothes for the ferry crossing. Even the cabins are cold this time of year." He put down his cup. "I'll give you Peter's address in London. He'll know some place safe, and he won't ask questions."

"Why don't you come, too?" she asked. "See Peter."

"Rather go south, Italy, Crete," Willem said. "I have to think."

"Think fast. Tomorrow—" Heather wanted to say that Brett would find her by tomorrow, but a fit of coughing stopped her and caused her to drop her cup.

"You contagious?" Willem patted her on the back and offered her water. "What've you got? Your eyes are yellow."

Chapter 12

Taylor

Arriving at the Grants Hotel in Harwich, Nichols parked the Jaguar in back. Taylor opened the car door and offered to carry Elias van den Dolder's valise. He permitted it.

"Find your way to the upstairs dining room," Nichols said. "I'll be with you shortly."

Taylor and Elias climbed to a small paneled room with floor-length, heavy, dark red drapes. Taylor admired the vastness of the high-ceilinged room and would have thought it uncomfortable but for the fire that burned behind a grate, warming the air, if not the whole room.

Elias rubbed his hands before it and then sat at one of the three tables, placing the portfolio before him, fingering its strings. Taylor kept his back to the fire, so rare and wonderful to have real flame from wood and not from an oily, electric heater. He placed Elias's suitcase at his feet. Nichols would tell him when and what to do with it.

"I ordered the eggs poached." Nichols carried in coffee and toast on a tray. "May take a minute. They'll likely have to find the recipe in a cookery book. It's all right to show emotion, Taylor. You're not on parade."

"Come and sit down," Elias said to him. "We'll all be friends together. Tell me, have you ever been to Holland?"

Taylor shook his head. "Spain. Went on a holiday, years ago."

The pubkeep arrived with three English breakfasts, the eggs and bacon steaming, the fried tomato plopped on top, and more toast. A beige cozy encased a teapot. A cream pitcher and bowl of sugar cubes sat on the bottom rung of the trolley.

Elias cut his food into tiny bits before eating it. He sipped his cooling coffee. Taylor kept up with Nichols in a seeming race to end the meal first, reaching for toast with a snap of fingers and spooning the jam with clinks against the edges of the jar. They used their cutlery like small, black-handled spears: cutting, stabbing, scraping.

Nichols set down his knife and fork, sat back, and breathed out satisfaction.

Now, Taylor thought, *he'll tell me the next part of this excursion.*

"We need quiet." Nichols pulled his glasses from his jacket pocket. "Get yourself lost for a few hours." He offered Taylor the car keys. "Oh, put the valise on the table, would you?"

Taylor zipped his coat as he stood. So much for feet by a warm fire and the lazy afternoon that he expected. He placed the case on the table with its handle toward Elias.

"Sergeant," Elias said. "He means, 'Have a good time.'"

Taylor smiled and shook his hand. Nichols did not look up.

"You shouldn't scatter people like mice whenever

you're done with them," Elias said, as Taylor closed the
door.

Chapter 13

Elias

Elias unlocked his valise and pulled out a file from the portfolio. Flipping the file open, he withdrew a photograph and handed it to Nichols.

"What have you for me? Don't fret about Taylor. He understands, smart lad." Nichols shrugged. "Though he has the devil's own luck for finding trouble. Stitched up three times this year." He wiped his bifocals, holding the photo close, studying a spider tattoo on the white man's forearm.

Elias stood, stretched, and walked to one of the windows. He drew the drapes only to find thin voile panels clinging to the misty glass. He dreamed of a view from his own front window, one from long ago. There she rode: a young woman, his Alise, pedaling her yellow bicycle, a bouquet of sunflowers in her basket, the shadows trailing her, kerchief falling back, and strands of her blonde hair slipping from her braid.

"Sorenson kept duplicate slides of all his work in a safety deposit box at his bank," Elias said, turning from the window. "He left nothing to chance. He made some very bad enemies. Petty dealers, but they are often the most vindictive."

He tried to keep his mind on the case, but he was so tired.

"Sorenson?" Nichols asked. "Your informant?"

"Dead now." Elias couldn't say murder. "Cuts, bruises, fractures, followed by a free fall from his fourth-floor studio window. Garden variety sort of death." He moved back to the table and sat in his chair.

Nichols slid the picture toward him. "Acrobatic, was it?"

"A genuine '*Nadia Comaneci*,'" Elias said. "No witnesses. Team assigned to the flat got called away on another disturbance."

Nichols sat forward in his chair. "Convenient."

"Not unlike yours, the hanging on the bridge. A banker about to be indicted suddenly turns up dead." Elias handed Nichols a set of Sorenson's sketches. "But Sorenson's American. That always makes for trouble. Someone, probably a lawyer, will arrive asking, 'How could this happen?'" He rolled his shoulders, but the stiffness remained and pained him. "And your banker? Any claims on his person, his money?"

Nichols lined the sketches in a row, blinking, baffled. "No one's claimed the body. His employer hasn't even made inquiries into his disappearance, and McIness has been missing for a week," he said. "I expect the case'll be cold and shelved by New Years. We picked up Peter Jurg as you suggested, but we've gotten nothing out of him."

"I'll get something out of him. Dutchman to Dutchman, he'll talk." Elias lifted the tea cozy and felt the pot. He poured tea for himself and offered some to Nichols. He declined.

Nichols cleaned his glasses, his usual delaying tacit. He examined a drawing. "All these sketches are of the same woman?"

"Heather Hiscocks. She's one of yours, English." Elias turned one of the drawings over and pointed to penciled notations. "Feel the paper. The back and front have different coatings. Experiments, we guess, or why else hide them inside his mattress?"

"Sorenson gave his work a signature coating?" Nichols fingered the paper. "Wouldn't that be counterproductive? Make a fake easier to spot?"

"The coating mimics aging," Elias said. "Increases authenticity. But if we have the formulas, we could test the work and match it with work that Sorenson did at the Courtauld and in Aberdeen." He rubbed his eyes under his glasses. They stung with the grit of no sleep.

Nichols picked up the evidence bag and stared at it. "Aberdeen?"

Elias flipped one of the drawings. "The University of Aberdeen. Sorenson was sent there by the Courtauld as a favor." He produced a contract and indicated the signatures. "Sorenson was given three weeks to clean a manuscript and to repair it. He took three weeks, but the work took two. The other week he spent with her."

"Don't they usually send a team of restorers?" Nichols asked.

Elias chuckled. "Sorenson was a team of restorers. And an entrepreneur, sold things on the side. That's what got him into trouble."

Nichols cleaned his glasses with a plaid handkerchief. "Paintings?"

"Paintings, drugs, things, even cars when he had a buyer. His habit kept him pretty busy." Elias opened the valise and pulled out a manila envelope. He set a photo of the Archangel Gabriel before Nichols. "Recognize this? It was found in Sorenson's studio. Part of an altarpiece stolen two months ago."

Nichols shook his head no. "We're looking for a Dali."

"Everyone's looking for a Dali," Elias said. "But it's this altarpiece that interested Sorenson. He specialized in Renaissance works." From the valise, he took an evidence bag containing a piece of canvas depicting that same archangel. "This is all that remains of that altarpiece which hung in an Italian chapel for five hundred years. I found this scrap on the floor of Sorenson's studio."

Nichols fingered the painted surface. "This is the original? You're certain? Sorenson was a forger."

Elias put one hand on the back of Nichols's chair then patted his shoulder with the other. "I'm certain."

Nichols smiled. "Are you certain he's the thief?"

"No," Elias said. "I can blame Sorenson as he's not alive to argue. But, you know, Catholic churches are always open."

"Not anymore, they aren't," Nichols said. "We've sent warnings."

Elias laughed, He imagined heralds in medieval dress, reading out decrees on the church steps and bolting vestries with locks the size of coconuts. He saw balding priests Sunday mornings tottering up stone steps with a jumble of keys as rain battered them and wind ripped at their surplices.

"Understand me." Nichols touched his friend's hand. "We do need some legal standing for a successful prosecution."

Elias laughed louder, a young man's noise, a jangle from crotch to brain. "Legal standing? Vernon, when did you ever need legal standing? You're a commander. You order it, and it happens, like this meeting, this breakfast, this room."

Nichols flushed. "Until some commission begins an investigation of my department." He sat back from the table. "This isn't the first time money and art have gone missing. And with Blunt disgraced, all his associates are suspect. Every week there's another memo from a sub-committee, another request for twenty-year old files."

Elias put both hands on the table and eased himself into a chair. "You're not Blunt's associate. I'm not his associate. The art we're following are forgeries made after the originals were stolen."

"Blunt authenticated forgeries," Nichols said.

"Yes, and Blunt was a specialist in Renaissance art, the same as Sorenson." Elias pointed to the scrap of canvas. "But this was stolen two months ago. Nothing to do with Blunt. Please, Vernon. Three years, I've devoted to this case, to the money and drugs and crates going in and out of Amsterdam. This operation we have to shut down, evidence or no evidence. We don't want more forgeries flooding the market."

Nichols frowned. "To be sold through the Chelsea Estates Gallery. You know, they labeled the artwork 'household goods' so they could avoid custom duties? How many agents do you think X-ray 'household goods'?"

Elias took two bank statements from the portfolio. "These are bank statements from an account in the Antilles. We've identified the account holder as Paul Hutchinson of Putney, England. Notice the sums and the regularity of sums. What solicitor gets that kind of money?" He crossed his legs at his ankles.

Nichols examined the papers. "Five thousand pounds every week? Hutchinson might call it a retainer. But that begs the question: a retainer for what?"

"For running money through his office which keeps its accounts in William McIness's bank. The transactions are on these tapes." Elias pulled several small, square cardboard boxes from the suitcase. "Now will you bring the Hutchinsons in for questioning?"

Nichols shook his head. "Hines wants to haul them in. But I say, let them stew. They're not going to flee. They may close their accounts, sell their shares in McIness's bank, but they've yet to feel guilty." He stretched his arms above his head and then dropped them into his lap. He began to yawn and relax as if drugged by hot food. "They'll divest within the month."

Elias took a telegram from his coat pocket. Nichols read it and reread it while Elias sat quietly. Then Nichols refolded it and returned it to him without comment.

Nichols packed the files and tapes into the valise.

"We need the tapes and logs from McIness's bank and the stock exchange to follow the money as it passes through accounts in smaller and smaller amounts," Elias said. "That's how it's done. The account numbers are encoded in hexadecimals. We'll need an expert."

Nichols clicked the suitcase closed. "Do you know one?"

"I know that Taylor isn't one," Elias said. "Why is he here?"

Nichols pushed his chair away from the table, away from Elias, the screech of wood against wood. "Bodyguard," he said. "I need Hines and Kitner to busy themselves with Taylor and leave me free to investigate them." He shifted his jaw unnecessarily. His skin pinked with anger. "Hines. His voice is enough to anger me for three days. And don't ask me why I don't fire him. It's not in my power. Arrest him I can, but not without more evidence than computer code."

He walked to the window and back, taking hold of the back of the chair he'd just vacated. "Hines rushed in upon me at the Chelsea gallery, all full of news he was, as if Peter Jurg and his heroin habit mattered. Elias." He lowered his voice. "Hines has taken the bait. He's following Taylor. An innocent man wouldn't bother about a subordinate."

Elias looked at his cuff. "I did what you asked. When Hines called me, I told him how Willem Jurg laundered money through his club and how he paid for his brother, Peter, to live in London." He held his cup out for more tea.

"Hines wants my job," Nichols opined and obliged, watching as the dark tea filled Elias's cup. "He thinks the Jurgs are his ticket to promotion. International case, murder, stolen art. A successful prosecution would be a feather in his cap, so he thinks."

Elias held the cup to his lips. "Hines is a bully. He'd never make commander, even if he weren't a criminal."

"So Jean tells me," Nichols said. "She worries about me, her wifely prerogative. She expects to see you, the boys as well."

Elias shivered as he drank. "I expect to see her and them." He hadn't wanted to come, but now that he was here, he must make Vernon listen. He missed Beers, his loyalty, his understanding, and all their silly jokes.

Nichols stretched and smoothed his clothes. "Tomorrow."

Elias stood abruptly and then tried to catch his teacup before it smashed on the floor. "Today, Vernon. For the family you love, Jean, the boys, that harmless sergeant of yours, we must make arrests before anyone else is killed." He had lost patience with his friend. He knew he'd not persuaded Vernon to act and he wanted to know why. Why was Vernon holding back?

"There's been no pot shots, Elias. Not at me, not at Taylor."

Elias said, "Listen to the messages." He reopened the

valise and dropped one of the tape boxes on the table. "No threats, no warnings. Sorenson alive one day and dead in the street the next."

Nichols cocked his head. "What would you have me do?"

Elias tossed a glossy color print at Nichols. "Notify the harbor authorities, the rail authorities, the airlines. We need this woman."

Nichols caught the portrait of a young woman, pretty, blonde, exiting a bank. He squeezed the heavy paper between thumb and finger. He stared at the evidence lined up in the case. "Taylor should be back soon." He dropped the picture into the open valise. "You explain it all to him. He'll stiffen like an old maid if I start spinning fairy stories about femmes fatales from Amsterdam."

Elias shook his head, his breath visible. "Have you adopted this policeman? Is he your protégé?"

Nichols took a turn before the weakening fire. "No, but you didn't hear Hines that night at Blackfriars. He interrupted Taylor repeatedly, digging into him, threatening him. That kind of hostility has to be wondered at. What threat could Sergeant Taylor of Southwark pose to Hines?"

Elias watched Nichols move about the room. "Threats could be to you. Think of that. Think of your family." He spoke more loudly than he intended. "Send Jean and the children to Wales. Do this now before anything hits the papers."

Nichols stopped at Elias's shoulder. "I can't send Evan anywhere. He barely speaks to me. He's dating McIness's PA. You know that's not accidental. Bloody fool. How do I tell him?"

Elias shifted in his chair. "How do you tell Taylor he's bait?" The fire burned low, and the room grew cold.

"Doesn't he deserve a chance to protect himself? You said Hines already has it in for him."

"Taylor doesn't need warning," Nichols said. "He's been a target all his life. You should see his medical records—stitches, cracked ribs, dislocated shoulder. He must have a 'kick me' sign on his forehead."

"The mark of Cain?" Elias remarked.

Nichols cleaned his glasses with his handkerchief. "More likely those great girlish eyes of his."

Elias had not seen his friend look so weary. "You expect Hines to come after Taylor?" He desired more tea but thought it not wise to ask. He'd already asked for too much.

"Absolutely." Nichols looked at his watch. "Hines will reveal himself to Taylor. It's inevitable." He clasped his hands behind his back. "Then we'll know with whom Hines is working. We know he's not savvy enough to move money through half-a-dozen banks. He couldn't type a report without jamming his fingers between the keys. And Kitner is a bloody fool."

Elias fidgeted, rubbed his shoes on the carpet beneath his chair. "Kitner has computer access. You sent him to the school yourself."

"So he could put my files onto the main frame, not steal from banks," Nichols said, He looked at the fire and the thin smoke it was producing.

Elias looked up. "We're back to the girl."

Nichols flicked an imaginary epee. "The wee minx, the elusive pimpernel: Miss Heather Hiscocks."

Elias forced his feet together as if they could disobey him. "We've no bargaining chip with her now that Sorenson's dead."

"We have her life," Nichols stated. "She might be willing to part with some of it, but not all. We can invoke the Protection Against Terrorism Act and see if she finds her voice."

Elias pursed his lips. "It's a risk. She may tell us nothing."

"She'll give us the codes." Nichols blinked as if he saw numbers before him. "And she won't give them to Hines, and we will recover those millions gone missing from the Bank of London. I'll not retire out of shame. I'll not be questioned by the Home Office and be found wanting."

Time to speak of other matters, Elias knew. It was not time to slice into old scars, or bring up the war, and its aftermath of inequalities.

"We've been working on this too long," Nicholas said, recognizing Elias's impatience, his voice losing its crack of command. "Listen to me. I sound like I'm quoting scripture and, lord knows, I'm as god-fearing as a horse's arse."

Elias avoided his old friend's eyes and looked at the worn tabletop, his two hands upon it, his skin loose over swollen knuckles. He folded his hands the right over the left and prayed for comfort. *Lift them up. I have lifted them up to the Lord.*

Nichols poked the charred logs, seeking flame. "We need to get out of here. You're freezing. Where's that pubkeep?"

The pubkeep hurried in, aggrieved. "Sorry to interrupt, sir," he said. "You've a call from a detective. He says it's important. You can take it in the bar."

Chapter 14

Heather

The bedroom door creaked and woke her. Heather elbowed herself upright in the lumpy bed, looking around wildly for a way out of the room. What room was she in? Not the hostel, then where?

A click of a light switch followed by the aromas of onions, stew, coffee, and cigarettes. Then the, lesser smells of tea and toast as Willem set a heavy tray before her. She flopped down, relieved, her heart slowing.

She saw her yellow fingertips as she pulled the tray closer, eyed the orange juice, jam, and butter, and mouthed her thanks. She craved the food. She felt good, not feverish.

Willem nodded, unshaven, unwashed, anxious, his blond hair in a ponytail. He drew the drapes, and sunlight tumbled through the window. He pulled a portable heater toward the bed.

Heather enjoyed this breakfast in bed, a reminder of Sundays with Sorenson, his lecturing, a cigarette between his fingers and a brush behind one ear. She would remember him that way, with an April sun filling the windowsill of their kitchen, their green cotton curtains rippling, the ones she made. She could almost hear the sizzle of butter: Sorenson making pancakes in the shapes of dolphins and whales, kissing her between batches, excitedly satisfied by a piece of work, now sold.

The burning urge for revenge against Brett dulled somewhat, due to the calming effect of the fresh light striking the white bedroom walls, the white duvet covering her, and the food before her. She had Willem to work on a little longer. He didn't seem quite ready to abandon his club and rush off with her to parts unknown.

Willem sat on a stool, cigarette smoke spiraling up. Heather thought to applaud, but his agitation quelled her. She wondered where he'd slept, if he'd slept. The red edges of his brown eyes suggested otherwise. She coughed, her breath stale and burning in her mouth and throat. The tea soothed and warmed, but she needed more help than this.

She put her palms together and begged for a cigarette.

Willem shook his head "You're ill. You get tea and toast. I get coffee and cigarettes." He flicked ash into a small shell. Smoke ascended.

Heather pressed her fingers to the inside of his wrist. She felt the pulsing in his veins. "Brett's not coming," she said with an effort.

"No?" He lifted his head, stubbing out his cigarette. "It's in the papers, Sorenson's death. Cut, tortured, thrown through his own window to the ground, like trash, like an empty bottle. You think it can't happen to me, to you?" He crossed his legs and stared at the floor.

She sipped the stew, licking her cracked lips, the red of the tomatoes too close in color to blood.

Willem moved closer to the bed, reached for the coffee cup. "I'll drive you to Rotterdam. No one will look for you there." He swigged the espresso. "You take the ferry to Dover. I go south to Spain."

She should have stayed in Zurich, then she pushed that thought from her brain. She couldn't have stayed there, not with Brett trailing her. She had luck catching the train when she did. That was what she had to think. Willem had sheltered her. He could have packed up, cleared out, after his club closed. He could have taken that trip to England, to stay with Peter in Fulham. He'd mentioned it enough times.

He chewed a piece of her toast, his eyes fixed on her. "You remember Marta? The midwife?" he asked. "I called her. She told me to take you to a hospital. She guesses pneumonia."

"There are hospitals in Dover," Heather said.

"That's what I said." He lit another cigarette, waved the smoke away from Heather. "Did I get an earful? Contagious, spread by coughing, casual contact, endangering hundreds of people on the ferry."

"You've known Marta a long time," she said. "She'll forgive you."

"Not enough to come with me," Willem said. "She hates Spain."

Heather drank the orange juice, the chilled sweetness a marvel. Willem's cooking brought as many people to the club as the music. She thought how one forgets, what one forgets. She rested her head on the pillow, stretching to pour more tea into the cup, sweating, feverish again.

ⲉⲟⲉⲟ

She woke again, surprised she'd been sleep. The tray had been removed and the drapes drawn. The bedside lamp illuminated Willem.

He held a framed charcoal sketch, one that she recognized. It was that nude drawing of herself, Sorenson's favorite. He'd kept in his bedroom. It worried her to see it, especially in that ridiculously huge, heavy frame.

"Sorenson left it here," he said. "To brighten the place."

She gulped air and pushed the words out. "Kept it on an easel by his bed. Where he could see it." Coughing, twisting half-out of the bed, she mimed for pen and paper. She wrote *remove frame*. Willem read, stared at her and read again. She beat the bed with her fists and mouthed, "Do it. Now. Please."

He shrugged and fetched a toolbox. Carefully removing the wire, he tore off the brown paper, pried off the thin cardboard and stood back. There hung a pelt of hundred dollar bills, arranged across the width of the backing, ten across, and twelve down, at least three layers deep. Willem paced to the window, raving in Dutch.

Heather tugged at a bill. Lightly glued, it fluttered from her fingers, so she pulled several by their edges. They tumbled, forming green streaks on the slatted floor. Damnable Sorenson, what else had he hidden? The police had his flat cordoned off so she couldn't check, though ill as she was, she'd never make it there and back.

"Stop," Willem said sharply. "Leave it alone. Do you know how much is there? More than I bank in months. We need a plan. Anyone hears of this, Brett'll arrive in a flash." He grabbed the picture—more dollars spun in the air.

Heather laughed at the sight then covered her mouth as she coughed. She wrote on the paper again—*wire it.* That's how she had done it. Wired it herself, same amount to five different accounts, over a succession of five days. In Zurich, no questions asked. Dutch banks might be different but not by much. And if the right amount of money began appearing in the accounts, maybe Brett would stop chasing her, maybe forget about her. That was a faint hope, but it was a hope.

Chapter 15

Taylor

Taylor drove north, away from Harwich, the sea, and those secret talks at the hotel. Rain splatted off the wipers. Traffic lessened. He enjoyed the straightforward emptiness and turned down an unmarked lane. A single blaze of sunlight struck across the road, illuminating the brown bark of the trees, the dripping leaves, and two sets of black skid marks.

Crashed into an oak, a black Jaguar jutted into the road.

Taylor slammed on the clutch and brake. The XJ12 lurched to a stop behind the newer model, its doors wide open.

As he approached, half expecting the vehicle to vanish, mud oozed over his shoes and patches of ice gleamed underfoot. He called out as he saw boot heels to the right of the driver's door. Bracing himself against the bent hood, he gazed at the body of a man lightly clothed in a gray suit. Arms and legs splayed, the corpse flattened the grass beside the car, the clothing crimson with blood.

Taylor bent but didn't touch. He stepped away, awash in doubt. He doubted the sight, doubted he could explain it without getting it all wrong. He missed his notebook and his pen.

He steadied himself, scanned the area, wanting a weapon, his eyes narrowing against the fading light. He studied the footprints—their size, width, and depth in the boggy earth. He noticed the litter of leaves, red, and yellow, blown about the body when it had fallen.

Taylor punched 999 on the car phone, identified himself, and the emergency. He rattled off the landmarks he recalled, looked at his watch as he hung up. Radio-1 played a song he hated. He didn't call Nichols.

Two constables arrived and established a perimeter. They patted Taylor down, took his billfold, examined his ID, and measured his shoes. He didn't lie, but the car registration caused them to wonder what he was doing sixty miles from home in another man's Jag on a beastly day of heavy rain and icy mist. Between telling and retelling his story, he hunkered in the passenger seat, his greatcoat buttoned tight.

The talking made him thirsty. He thought of the Grant's Hotel with its old-fashioned ivory taps, the red leather booths, the red-patterned carpet, and the golden lager, all colors never seen in Emile Glanz's gallery. Glanz favored pale grays and greens, even in the back rooms, the storage closets, bins, and file folders. Taylor thought of his unfinished search of those folders and Glanz now dead on the wet, green grass.

He cranked the seat flat, shielded his eyes from the emergency vehicles' vibrant red lights. The medical team set up its marquee.

A plump man squeezed into the driver's seat. His soft belly compressed against the steering wheel. All the metal on his raincoat dinged as he faced Taylor.

He beamed as he enjoyed Taylor's grim surprise. "So what am I to think?" Hines asked. "Two sets of skid marks, two cars, a dead man, and you out for a lark? No maps, no picnic, no girl." An exasperated shake of his head, hair dark and very wet.

"I didn't kill him," Taylor said. He rolled the seat up, feeling at a physical disadvantage to Hines.

"Obviously," he said. "Not unless you hosed yourself off afterward and melted down the gun."

Taylor clipped each word. "I saw an accident and stopped."

A crinkle of plastic as Hines leaned his wide shoulders toward Taylor. "We both know who he is," he said. "I saw it in your face when the ME moved him. Not that you could see me with all the lights in your face. Come on, speak up. Tell me."

"Emile Glanz." Taylor remembered the man's elegant clothes, his impatient manner, his hurried steps into a back room when the front door opened and Hines and Kitner entered. "Gallery owner in Chelsea."

"Get his home address from him, did you?" Hines almost sang. "Having it off with him, are you? Naughty weekend turned nasty?"

Taylor remained mute, stared at his knees with sweet idiocy. His left leg began to shake, not from cold. Shame, the great ball-buster, gay love, the career-ender, the lie that branded.

Bullies like Hines never grew up, and nobody needed them.

Taylor knew this game, this probing, but he didn't answer. He didn't describe the drive to the Harwich dock, or the warm fire at the hotel. He forced from his mind the memory of the taste of the milky coffee and the sight of the Dutchman sipping his with the edge of the cup to his lips, as if it were a rare delight.

Hines draped one arm over the steering wheel. "What are you really doing down here? It's okay, you can tell me."

Taylor shifted in the seat, his voice loud. "Full cooperation with local authorities," he said, "is our duty and our pleasure."

"Full cooperation? Don't make me laugh, Sergeant Taylor, if that's truly your name and rank. Where'd Nichols find you, eh? What's the setup? We follow you while he earns a knighthood cracking the case?" Hines's knees bumped the steering wheel as he sat up. "Get Nichols on the line and don't tell me you don't know where he is."

Taylor got the hotel's number from directory inquiry. He and Hines took turns talking to Nichols. Their brief exchanges interspersed with "yes, sir, right away, sir, of course, sir."

Hines glared and clicked the phone off with punctuating force. "I don't care whom he knows at Downing Street, or Westminster, I'll have you down here for the inquest, the assizes, everything." He squeezed out of the driver's seat. "You'll talk."

Breathing deeply, Taylor stayed put as ordered. He listened to Radio-1 again, bobbing his head to the bass line of the pop tune, imagining the scolding to come and those questions in the white room with the tape recorder. How many hours would he have to spend detailing the finding of the body, the road, the rain, and the dark day?

He wondered what Elias van den Dolder would make of all this, with his untroubled air and his friendly questions. He was an odd a man, carrying that worn suitcase with its bamboo handle and using his knife and fork so precisely.

Nichols would have to bring van den Dolder to Scotland Yard, and he'd be very cross about that. He'd scowl and lower his voice, peering over his glasses at Taylor. This would be a dressing down right out of primary school.

Elias would play the academic, claiming he had no jurisdiction and no wish to intrude, while he'd comb through evidence bags, prod constables, and order tests. But it would all be a show for Hines and Taylor the dancing monkey.

Taylor watched the widening gap in the clouds. He heard the plunk of rainwater as an accusing wind ripped drops from branches and leaves, flinging them against the cars.

He wondered what Hines was doing in Harwich. Following Nichols? Or maybe, some business of his own?

It was not reasonable that Hines happened along so conveniently, so ready to handle the murder of Emile Glanz. What other murders had he handled? William McIness's death by hanging?

Chapter 16

Elias

Nichols and Elias left the Grants Hotel and met a local constable at the door. They sped out of Harwich in a police vehicle, not comfortable. Noise of the town ceased as the road grew shadowed with ancient trees: a haunted land where animals had burrowed and hollowed out the roots of oaks and beech, a dour country with damp that seeped through rock and wall, chilling the bone.

Elias regarded this trip as another delay and more wasted resources. He wanted Nichols to get the subpoenas, order arrests, and fill the jails. He daren't say this, crammed in the back of the car, the black portfolio across his knees, a beefy patrolman, Brader by name, answering Nichols's questions about an accident not involving Nichols's car, not caused by Taylor, and not any business of theirs that Elias could determine.

When they halted amid emergency vehicles, a plump man opened the passenger door and introduced himself to Elias as DS Hines. Elias knew the voice, but didn't want to know the man. He didn't leave the car and didn't follow Nichols, who rushed into the scene, scorching a swathe though the huddled men.

Doors slammed, leaving Elias alone. No cup of coffee to warm him, no Beers to joke with. A tingle pulsed down his left arm, a hot pain, terrible and strange. He pulled his arm to his chest as his jaw quivered. His mouth opened and shut uncontrollably His teeth scratched his tongue. His eyes closed as he tumbled face-first onto the seat.

A wet cloth touched his face, a voice buzzed in his ear—not friendly, demanding, insistent. Elias blinked, his face still aching, his hands empty, lying on his back in the car, feet sticking out the door.

Nichols looked over the driver's seat. "How is he?"

"Coming round, sir," the insistent voice said.

"Elias," Nichols said. "You fainted. Can you sit up? The ME wants a quick look at you. That, or it's off to hospital."

Elias struggled as Taylor helped him upright. The ME's cold hands prodded him, stretched his eyelids, and took his pulse, annoying him. He was old, couldn't the ME see that? Couldn't an old man fall asleep without a retinue of doctors poking him with stethoscopes?

He didn't ask from whose flask he drank or whose brandy he savored. He tried not to listen to the argument Nichols had with the ME. Elias heard the word "endanger," and he knew that the doctor was justifying his diagnosis, using legal terminology to impose his will. But Nichols was not one to be goaded or riled.

"Brader?" Nichols called. "We're off to Glanz's cottage. We've seen all we can here. Do know you the way to Gulls Haven?"

Brader drove too fast for Elias who minded the skidding turns and slippery road. He objected to being tossed about in the back seat. Beside him, Taylor sat, all bone, woolly, unfeathered, flightless, an emu out of the egg. Elias watched him, the scenery no longer visible as the sun had set. So quickly, thoroughly bleak these English winter afternoons, a black paste that smoothed road, tree, and sky into a level gloom.

Nichols twisted his head, telling Elias, "Emile Glanz. Forced off the road, and shot. We'll have a look round his house. Then home."

Few vehicles passed them. Elias felt homesick: no smell of the sea, no brightly-lit barges on the canals, no decorated bridges, no busy cafes and, most of all, no Adjutant Beers to speak to him of common pursuits. The night ferry would leave without Elias. He touched his watch, admiring its brass stem and its leather strap. The engraving of his wedding date hidden against his skin.

A two-story house fronted by a paved driveway, potted plants by the tall door, rectangles of light from windows shaded by huge gables.

Brader opened the car door for Nichols while Elias eased himself out of the back seat, the clammy air boring into his joints. The ground icy, slick, treacherous for his arthritic knees.

Nichols pulled off his gloves, stuffed them into his coat pocket as he crossed the threshold. "Assist him, Taylor. The journey's tired him."

Taylor stepped to Elias, his big head bent.

Nichols dashed up the stairs with Brader in tow.

Uneasy, still, shaken, Elias grumbled at his own weakness. "I'm not a cripple." He was troubled by this peculiar place. "Stairs?" He groaned and heaved himself up the steps, with Taylor close behind, unspeaking.

The studio's low hanging lights shone on every broken canvas, on spilled paint, torn chairs, and smashed shelves. Elias's heart jumped in his chest, making him lurch and his breath noisy. Taylor steadied him, but he slipped from the sergeant's grip. As his knees failed, Elias focused his eyes on the rough cloth of a sofa. He flopped on it as the prickly cold receded. Taylor brought him a round pillow.

"Everything wrecked," Elias said. "Amsterdam again."

Taylor didn't answer and helped him lie down.

"Brett." He croaked, his lips tight. "He slashes. That's his way."

He cringed, stiff with sadness, unable to rise, unable to finish his task, which was to get home. He must first finish this case and set the future in order as he has done for years. Out-foxed, out-maneuvered, a flop, aged and dim, he remembered the nicknames bestowed on him by the English pilots in the days of the war: *prophet, Methuselah, diamond-eye* for the many facets he saw in word and voice. Now *washout, too late by half, past-it.*

Nichols perched on the sofa's arm, his face fierce. "I don't think there's much for us to do here. A rat's nest."

Elias gave a slow nod, his eyes blurred under the harsh light.

"We'll get Olivar and Lake here," Nichols said. "They'll find this more exciting than photographing labels and waybills."

Chapter 17

Heather

Amsterdam in its soggy morning clothes. Rain plunked on the casement of the one window in the plain bedroom where Heather woke.

Two figures at the window, kissing, Willem and Marta.

Heather looked from the couple to the corners of the room. In the dim light, she saw shapes, no portrait, no frame, and, more significantly, no money. She shifted the bedclothes and slid from the bed. She tumbled, elbows and knees bruising on the floor.

❧❦❧

Willem woke her with a slow shake. She was back in bed but not warm, her toes burned with cold, and her heart thumped. Her illness held her fast. She felt the pillow beneath her head and the blankets piled thick upon her. Late morning, she guessed, no rain, but she wasn't fit to travel.

Marta showed her a small bottle with tiny writing and a black stopper. "Three drops under the tongue every three hours," she said. "It'll break the fever." She smiled, her eyes wet with tears. Her blue sweater was a shade darker than her eyes. "Willem says you go to Rotterdam." She gulped as if she had more to say.

Willem laid his hand on Marta's shoulder. "Marta made you a special tea. Half a cup, twice a day." He handed Heather a white mug.

Marta touched his hand and their fingers entwined. "With honey, for the cough. Willem says we can't take you to a doctor. That would spoil your escape." She started to laugh. Willem kissed her on her brow.

Heather mouthed the word "Money?" the empty cup in her lap.

"I banked some of it," Willem said. "Marta will run the rest of it through the clinic. Don't worry. Sleep now. We have a plan."

∽∾∽

Marta startled her. How long had she slept? Night? Heather rolled onto her back. Marta sat and smoothed the bedclothes with thin fingers like Willem's. She laid a cool cloth on Heather's brow.

"You don't have to go," she said, her tan face soft under the one light. "Rotterdam or anywhere. I know you think it's dangerous here for you, for Willem, too, but we've hidden women before. Girls, too."

Heather propped herself against the headboard, listening.

Marta touched her hair, then her dress. "Dye the hair, different clothes. Big shoes to make you taller, it works."

Heather shook her head.

"I brought the dye." Marta pulled a glossy box from

the floor, set it on the bedside table. "We could do it now. You won't know yourself."

Heather took the package and stared at the young model on it with her heart-shaped face and bobbed chestnut hair. She read the words: *Covers gray. Lasting color.* She knew it was a good idea, but not good enough to keep her in Amsterdam. She returned the box to Marta, giving her a wide, potent smile. Marta hurried away. She returned almost immediately with towels, gloves, a pitcher, and a basin. "You can dye it a different color every month," she said. "No one will think anything of it."

Heather wrinkled her nose at the acidic smell as a thick goo plopped on her hair from the bottles Marta had been shaking. She lathered and rinsed, humming a very pleased little tune.

"Now we wait," she said. "You can tell me about Zurich. I haven't been there."

Heather pointed to her throat. She stifled a cough as she saw Marta blush at her mistake. She excused herself to make tea. Heather leaned forward on her elbows, eyed the closed door, and puzzled why they never left it open.

Marta carried in a tray. They sipped hibiscus tea and chewed red jelly biscuits, all of a palette, a theme. Heather watched as Marta crushed the packaging, gloves, and bottles. She set the whole mess ablaze in a metal bin and shuffled it toward the window. Fresh air tugged the black smoke out in a thinning string.

Heather stared in the mirror that Marta held. She flipped the ends of her now brown hair. Her eyebrows were dark and plucked high. They made her irises seem large and the whites less yellow. She clapped her hands to show that she was pleased, but she saw that Marta wanted a promise, not praise.

"You'll stay?" Marta asked.

The mirror lay face down in her lap. Her chin was up

and her voice brisk and hopeful. Heather shook her head no,

Marta bolted from the bed, her wool skirts snapped about her knees." We've looked after you. We gave you clothes and food. Willem's spent so much time on you." She waved the mirror up and around her head so violently that Heather scooted to the very edge of the bed. "I want Willem to stay here, with me, not go to Madrid. I don't care about the money, about the club. I don't care about you."

Heather eased herself to the floor and, crouching in the corner, hugged the pillow to her chest. She hoped it would soften whatever blow might come.

"Marta?" Willem entered the room with two bottles of beer in his right hand, and another in his left. "You finished?"

Heather looked straight at Willem, willing the anxiety to leave her face. This wasn't healing. This was captivity.

"What are you doing out of bed?" Willem asked.

Chapter 18

Taylor

Another Sunday, this time in Trafalgar Square and a morning bright in moments. It made Taylor's eyes smart and made him yearn for Spain, for its islands ablaze under a sun so hot that the air swirled like fire while strong-legged lizards and plaintive birds scurried into a teeming shade. Today the air stung, cold enough to snow as he stepped onto the St. Martin's in the Field's portico. The barricaded streets shone slippery from yesterday's drenching.

Well-rested for once, his body alert and strong, he enjoyed the new day, the uncomplication of guarding a crowd, supervising with his truncheon at his side. No Elias, no Nichols, no Hines, he was his own man today. He surveyed the square corner to corner. The police line extended from the south in a semi-circle, sweeping up the whole length of St. Martin's in the Field. Behind the police line, parked at angles for fast getaways, several emergency vehicles stood gleaming in a row.

He saw no white-coated personnel and guessed that

they waited inside the ambulances, eating Jaffa cakes and crisps.

He knew his mates were there and, like it or not, he'd join them later in The Prince of Wales. He'd gladly wash down some shepherd's pie with a Bass ale and suffer their censure. He'd let them have their say, complain about the overtime, the court time, and the added patrols. He'd smile as he was smiling now.

He adjusted his Kevlar vest, nightstick, and torch, sweating under the weight of the American-made riot gear. He cinched the chinstrap of his old-style helmet that his captain insisted his Southwark division wear to increase their visibility, and Taylor judged, their picturesqueness for TV viewers this December morning.

There on the steps of the church, he faced another impossible task: to guard Evan Nichols, the commander's son, amid this wobbly mob.

The protest had already swollen to a hundred thousand poster-waving marchers.

Taylor signed for a radio at the command desk that Kitner manned from a folding chair and table under the portico's shade.

Sergeant Kitner handed Taylor a pair of binoculars. "You'll need these."

He peered through the field glasses and searched the square for the best place to stand, out of the wind.

He lowered the glasses. "Horse guards at St James's?"

"Peace-niks," Kitner said. "Never know when they're going to go wild and rush the palace gates. Happened in Paris, you know, 1789."

Taylor gave him a little kick under the table. "July 1789. High summer and no food. These folks dine at wine bars. They'll run from the weather, to get out of it."

Kitner folded his hands atop a clipboard. "Heard you

met some locals in Harwich yesterday?" A typewriter clacked behind him.

Taylor wiped the binoculars' lens. "I took a drive in the country. My day off." Harwich, a place where he couldn't even get himself properly lost for an hour. No, he had to stop and play the Good Samaritan.

Kitner gave a grim laugh. "And in the gov's Jag. He's never so much as let me buff it. And I'm his assigned driver." He poked Taylor. "Did he ever tell you that?"

"He never mentioned it." Taylor focused on a solid clump of people lounging on the National Gallery's white steps. He wondered why they didn't go inside—where it was warm. He'd go inside if he had the choice.

"He's taken to you," Kitner said. "Never taken to me."

Taylor lowered the binoculars. "You want me to put in a good word?"

Name calling started behind Kitner as other constables shouted for their radios. "Get off." He handed a radio to another officer.

Taylor descended the stairs. As he slung the binoculars around his neck, he thought he was getting to like Kitner, or at least able to listen to him without flinching. Not that Taylor wanted to stand him a pint, but Taylor would heed Kitner when next they spoke. He wasn't that hard to work with, just touchy about Nichols.

The noise and numbers of the protestors increased, funneled phalanx-like from Pall Mall into the celebrated square. Every head seemed covered, and every hand gloved. This was not a day for displays of skin. Yet the marchers thrust out their chests and upraised their fists as they passed before the National Gallery. The few tourists who had braved the cold snapped their pictures and then darted into the National Gallery for warmth and security.

Taylor watched as people filled the square, celebrities in front, prams in the back, and the press in swarms. Their cameras clicked and trash circled in the blustery air. Bullhorns screeched as cheers echoed but, mercifully, no rain fell.

He took another look through the glasses. He saw Evan Nichols with Suzanne Cooper as the procession turned into the square. He began his slow trek toward them through the human river spilling over curbs and stairs toward the stage bright with banners.

Looking left as more cheers rose at the sight of the great stage festooned with anti-nuclear and pro-disarmament symbols, he picked up his pace as army-fatigue-dressed men, who had lounged decoratively on the National Gallery's steps, suddenly jumped from their perches and rushed into the square. Others in similar clothes pressed into the throng from a narrow alley at the side of the museum. They slashed at the marchers with sticks, chains, and pipes, bisecting the unarmed crowd. Protesters fell against each other, pushed forward by the marchers behind. As people were shoved into signposts and pillars, the cheers changed to screams and howls.

Taylor feared this kind of fighting, this wanton mauling stirred by rabid talk. He shoved his way toward to-day's assignment, Evan Nichols, but that lad didn't make it easy. No, he grabbed a skinhead by his jacket and punched the boy in the face, and that guy struck back with both fists before other marchers could grab Evan. The blow caused Evan to trip and Taylor to bump his way farther into the group. Slapping his nightstick against thighs and arms, he shoved with his hips to create space around him, angling for an unlikely rescue.

Surprisingly, he was aided by a civilian in a pea coat.

The man in his navy-blue coat shouted at the women beside him in the crowd. "Move." His great bulk shielded them from blows that caught Taylor in the stomach and chest. He sprawled over the frightened women, apologizing. Then he, too, urged them toward the empty space before the stage.

Someone grabbed his neck, caught his chinstrap, and snapped it. His head slapped into a shoulder, and he stumbled and fell, his helmet tumbling. His hands were stepped on as he tumbled between feet, now disorientated amid the pushing bodies, the air hot amid the milling crowd. He lunged upward as cries for help, police whistles and sirens assailed him. He inhaled deeply though his nose, keeping his mouth closed as dirt and blood swirled before him. He knew he must move these people to safety. He braced himself against the stocky man, back to back, the man calling to the women as to Santa's reindeers. "On Connie, on Carol, on Dana."

He and Taylor formed a wedge through the squealing crowd, their arms outstretched, waving and pushing. Together they herded the frightened women toward St. James's archway and assembled behind the horse guard's line. A horse's eye met Taylor's, but the horse's head did not move nor did the mounted guardsman stir.

More protestors staggered out of the square, panting, sobbing, some startled to find blood staining their hands, faces, clothes. In twos and threes, they funneled into St James's, Taylor serving as beacon and turnstile. His helmet was shoved into his arms. He placed it on his head with delighted command.

From the stage's PA system, a male voice urged calm, but the police line had already swept for its station before St. Martin's in the Fields. Reserve officers had dashed from behind the Horse Guards, elbowing apart determined combatants and arresting them. What voices could be heard were angry and shrill. Bodies bashed. Banners tore.

Taylor saw only the tops of heads, the up-swinging of truncheons and the fall of banners. He felt thankful to be out of the fray but angry to have failed his assignment. He'd had lost Evan Nichols.

Chapter 19

Elias

White always chilled Elias, the white, galling fluorescent lights that hung in police infirmaries like this one. He frowned at the white gowns, the white tubing, and the white half-moons of Peter Jurg's fingernails as Nichols and Elias stopped before Jurg's bed. Sweat beaded on the Dutch artist's brow. He knew he was quite the picture: his thin body, his swollen cheek, the blue bruise beneath his left eye and the white-knuckled grip he kept on the white bed sheets.

Jurg sniffed pointedly, making both a political statement and social commentary.

Elias sat on Jurg's bed, turning his back on Nichols. "Pray with me," he said in Dutch. "You can speak freely. My friend won't understand. *Unzen Vader in de hemelen, laot dienen name eheilegd worden. Our father who art in heaven. Hallowed be thy name.*" He bowed his head, took Jurg's smooth hands, and pressed them between his own. "You saw McIness last Saturday?"

Jurg answered in Dutch. "At his house. But we didn't

stay. He was afraid of the footprints by the windows." The young man closed his eyes and tilted forward. "That fat cop hit me. Look at my eye."

Elias pretended to continue the Lord's Prayer. "He won't hit you again."

"I don't know what it's all about," Jurg said. He opened his eyes, contrite. He struggled with Elias, crying out. "I want my sketchbooks. I want my paints."

Elias released Jurg's hands. "Look at these first."

Now came those black and white crime photos in the gray folder that Nichols carried under his arm. He pushed these toward Jurg, who shoved them into a pile on the side of the bed as if they stank.

Nichols set pictures of the murdered Emile Glanz in Jurg's lap. "Tell us about him," Nichols said, his Welsh lilt scratchy with impatience.

Jurg covered his face and rocked in the bed. The tubes bounced, the saline solution sloshing and the stand wobbling. Nichols restrained it.

Elias prayed for one credible, living witness. He gathered up the photos and handed them to Nichols. "Let's take a break," he said. "We'll get nothing but nonsense from him."

Nichols slipped the photos into the folder, tucked the folder under his arm, and picked up his coat from the other bed. He kept his back to Jurg. "We're probably late for some meal," he said. "I've been written up before for not giving my staff time for their dinner."

Elias smiled and thought of his little kitchen. He saw himself setting out for breakfast the yellow teapot with the loud whistle and the blue-edged dishes on the wide tablecloth, embroidered by his mother and given to him and Alise as a wedding present. It was still beautiful, not weathered like he was.

He looked at the door and became alarmed by the

loud footfalls that thudded in the corridor. He shuffled in short steps toward the head of Jurg's bed. He used Nichols as a shield though he was no bigger than Elias.

The door swung wide. Two men strode in, and Elias threw up his hands in excitement. He couldn't get the words out to say how pleased he was to see Lake and Olivar. The two officers returned his smile. He gripped each by the hand, smiling openmouthed.

"Sorry we're late, sir," Olivar said. He wore a shoulder bag and an odd grin on his tan face as he shook Elias's hand. "Traffic's at a standstill near the square. That rally. We had to double-back to Waterloo."

Nichols accepted the canvas bag as Jurg curled under the bedclothes, writhing away from the joyous greetings.

"Got a call on the way in," Lake said to Nichols. "We've really got something." He grinned, his chin tilted up as if to sing.

Olivar blurted, his usually smooth face sporting scruff, "You remember the money that Elias gave his informant? It's been deposited in an Amsterdam account, a maternity clinic, at least a portion of it. We're still missing some seventy thousand."

"Shut it down," Elias said, bumping Nichols. "Arrest them all. Tell Beers, only Beers. He'll get you a court order."

He took Lake's right hand in both of his, not encompassing it. The Irishman was too big to embrace, square and sturdy like the bookcase in Elias's bedroom. He thought of his books and their worn bindings instead of fraud and theft. He shifted his weight side-to-side, muttering in Dutch. No one listened as he had become the mad prophet from the country of ten-ton cheeses and fields of yellow tulips.

Yellow, his Alise's hair upon the white pillow in the hospice. Their son, ill with jealousy of the flowers, the fruit, and the visitors. A son like that: lean and devouring, like the calf in the prophesy, in the dream that frightened Pharaoh. Elias didn't want to go home to a son like Brett.

Nichols helped Elias with his coat. "Back to the office, both of you. Elias thinks we have enough evidence to make arrests. I think he might just be right."

Lake held the door, his outstretched arm forming an arch through which the others passed. "We've requested the bank's security footage," he said, as the infirmary door closed behind them.

"You haven't any bank statements from an Antilles bank in that bag of yours?" Elias leant on Lake's arm, Hunger added to his giddiness.

"No," Olivar said. "Wouldn't be of use to you anyway. No names, just numbers. Names we have to get from the Swiss. And you know how helpful they've been so far."

"I might be able to fix that," Nichols said. "I'm a commander of the Metropolitan Police, as Elias keeps reminding me."

"The British," Elias said, "are so perfectly gallant, so tactful. Always on about cooperation and concord."

"We have an empire to rule," Nichols said. His shoulders straightened.

Olivar whistled an annoying tune. Elias scowled at the noise.

They didn't go to Nichols's office but to the canteen. Nichols bought them sandwiches, fruit cups, and tea. Elias tried to hurry the others with taps of his silverware, but they chewed unhurriedly, dabbing their mouths with serviettes. Olivar and Lake returned to the line for trifle and coffee. Elias clicked his heels against the table leg. He whispered, "For pity's sake."

Nichols angled his chair from the table and stretched his legs. He fingered the cheap, white saucer.

Olivar dropped the tall spoon into the empty desert glass. "We started a random number generator last night to match possible account numbers and deposits in McIness's bank. We should have the results tomorrow." He dabbed cream from his mustache.

"We need access to the bank's data base," Lake said.

"I can get you that." Nichols sat up, his eyes fixed on Olivar. "Though I never said that, you understand?"

Olivar nodded. Lake nodded, too, setting his serviette on the table.

"Lake, let's phone the technology department from your office. It's not connected to the Yard's switchboard, and I can deny the call if inquiries are made." Nichols stood, not waiting for an answer. "Also, Lake." He quickened his pace to keep in step with the big man. "You might find some files from the Chelsea Estates Gallery in the boot of my car. They may be all we get now that Glanz is dead."

Elias followed Lake and Olivar into their temporary office with its light green walls, heating vent, and no clock. The soon-to-be corridor under the New Scotland Yard remodeling plan contained a desk, two computer terminals on a long table, a telephone, temporary shelving, boxes of files, and several blue plastic chairs. A confessional would have been more comfortable.

Lake placed the chairs about the table. "I'd say, 'Make yourselves comfortable.' But how's that possible? Austerity measures."

Elias was amused, his mind seeing the room as he had imagined it all those times he'd talked to Lake on the phone. His own office was not much different. Beers sat to the right, window to the left. But there was no window here, nor street noise.

This was a hideaway, a bit neglected for a hub of an international investigation, but who'd expect more for officers probing their own departments and their own superiors?

Nichols sat on the desk to dial the phone, watching, tapping on the blotter as the mechanism spun back into place with each number.

Elias watched Olivar remove his black leather gloves and waited to see if Olivar's hands were still as rosy brown as his cheeks and chin.

"Do you know what it's like spending all day talking to Swiss bankers?" Olivar asked, twisting his gloves. "Their bony chins pulled in and their eyes unblinking with the offense of being questioned. They pull their pudgy chests in and puff out their cheeks." He kicked one foot out at nothing. "You'd think I wanted to rip the arms off their grandmothers."

Elias unbuttoned his sodden coat.

Olivar said, "They only give us heat down here on the quarter hour, so you might want to keep your coat on."

Elias squirmed in the hard chair. "You've got the files from McIness's warehouse?"

Olivar pointed to the boxes. "Not much there."

"He means, we didn't find the Dali," Lake said. "We did find monthly exchanges between the gallery and McIness. Money was routed first through his company and then to his bank and then offshore, a typical pattern of money laundering."

"But there's a parallel pattern," Olivar said. "McIness sold shares in his own bank and in art objects. But the shareholders didn't know that art works were fake, and the bank kept a third of the cash it needed to pay all its debts. Wait until the Bank of London figures out the shares McIness sold them are worthless."

"But we can make a case?" Elias asked, his voice raised.

"A case, yes," Olivar said. "But against whom? McIness is dead, Sorenson, now Glanz. The bank execs won't admit anything, even if they know something. They'll write McIness off as a 'rogue operator.'"

"Sorenson's girl," Elias said, his hands clasped in his lap.

Nichols whispered, "Lake." He cupped his hand over the receiver. "You better take this. Something about a 'back door' you can use."

Elias remained quiet while Lake scribbled instructions onto a lined pad. A gruff roaring from the grate beside him. Heat puffed into the room, warming his legs. He jumped at the noise but welcomed the warmth.

Olivar rubbed his hands before the grate, dapper in his gold coat with its long darts down the back and padded shoulders. For Elias, Olivar seemed the "Aguilar," the eagle with his round bird eyes, flat brow, and slim nose. He was the tan crusader, afoot in the gray alleyways. He seemed zealous, contentious, a Steve McQueen scaling fences on a vintage motorcycle. There he goes, varooming through fields, pursued by hostiles.

Lake dropped the receiver into its cradle, fingers drumming.

"Out with it," Olivar said.

Lake frowned, discouraged. "We've got a way in, but I can't say what we'll get out of it. We may be reading code all night."

"Elias and I'll bring you coffee in the morning," Nichols said.

Lake gave a little jump as the phone rang. He relayed, "It's turned violent, the protest, sir. Kitner asks, could you come to the church, to St. Martin's in the Fields?"

Nichols asked, "Come to the church? What's that fool on about? They've plenty of men."

Looking upward, Lake answered Nichols's question. "I'm sorry, sir. Evan's been injured. He's being transported to hospital."

"Give me that phone," Nichols said, his jaws hardly moving.

Elias shivered as the heat clicked off. He wondered what injuries Evan has sustained as Nichols pressed the receiver hard against his ear, signaling quiet with his other hand.

Elias thought of Evan, the young man in the holiday snaps that Jean sent him: Christmas morning, his hand upon his brother's shoulder, the brown hair glossy with hair gel. What pictures would she send him now? Leg in a cast, stitches over one eye?

"Lake, you're with me." Nichols handed the phone to Olivar. "I want Taylor. You get him to tell you what happened."

Elias fingered the middle buttons of his coat.

"Elias, I know you want to come, but it's best that Olivar sees you home." Nichols took his coat. "We can start again tomorrow."

Elias sat and listened to Olivar as he spoke on the phone, admiring his phone manner, his sharp vowels, and his smooth face close to the notepad. Elias watched the heavy downward strokes of the pencil.

He enjoyed Olivar's competence. It gave Elias comfort. He cleaned his glasses with his handkerchief, not looking around, not wanting more harm to come to more people. Warnings, they were never of much use. Hurricanes blew, tornadoes spiraled, volcanoes erupted—no matter who said what to whom.

Chapter 20

Heather

Upstairs in his Amsterdam club, Willem regarded himself in a hand mirror. He stroked his new goatee dyed as black as his cropped hair. This made Heather laugh.

He sat beside her on the bed in brown wool trousers and a blue cardigan, the lunch tray on the floor. She took the mirror and admired her boyish cut. Twisting strands into pin curls, she felt prettier, fatigued, yes, but less pained in her chest.

Marta's drops were working, though Marta's distrust of her, Heather, had not abated.

Willem turned Heather's chin toward him, kissed her with his eyes open. "Why London?" he asked. "Why not Madrid?"

She inhaled between words. "Partners. They have to know." She became aware how the belt of her robe was slipping open, revealing her slimness in the too big pajamas. She coughed. "That I didn't take their money. And they're in London."

He lit a cigarette. "Would they hunt for you in Spain?"

"Yes," she said, sniffing the smoke. "They're not nice people. You don't want to meet them. Believe me."

He kissed her again, sweetly, not provocatively. "Come to Spain when you can. I won't be hard to find." Then Willem stretched out on the bed, crossing his legs at his ankles, relaxed, unhurried, and controlling.

She shuddered with anxiety. She stared at the doorknob and could feel her hand upon it. She had to get out. Willem may have a need to keep her here, keep her involved with Marta, but it didn't matter. She couldn't stay in this little room another night.

Willem flicked ash from his cigarette with two fingers. "Sorenson missed you. Surprised me, he did, going soppy after a few beers."

She stretched, her fists overhead. "Silly man, Sorenson."

Willem stood, "Think that will be me?" He put his cigarettes in his shirt pocket. "All sad and stupid in a Spanish disco?"

ഗ൭ഗ

As streetlights came on, he helped her don a backpack, a small one. Her few clothes filled it to the top, a sleeping bag filled the bottom. A wallet in her front pocket held the pound notes that Willem had purchased for her. He bought himself pesetas and traveler's checks, spending some of the cash that Sorenson left behind.

New leather boots made her three inches taller and clumsy. Wobbly, woozy, she aimed herself toward the open door before walking. He turned out the bedroom light, and she took no backward look. She had trouble keeping up with Willem, who was still taller. Down the stairs they clumped, and it was goodbye Amsterdam, goodbye Marta.

She sat shotgun in his green delivery van as he pulled into traffic, joining the rush-hour queue out of town. He angled his vehicle within the rumbling wake of a lorry. She swung the wing window out. Their breath formed a clinging fog on the windscreen. She stayed mute, relishing the cold as an adventure after the many days in bed.

He pushed in the electric lighter, hugging the steering wheel as he pulled a cigarette from the pack. "Marta tells me Spain is dangerous for women. Says she doesn't want to live there. That I'll have to come back."

"You want that?" Heather asked.

"Won't know 'til I get to Madrid." He laughed. "Always the way, my mother says. You want what you don't have."

He pounded on the dash. With a click, the heat streamed up their arms. She wiped the window with her old scarf. She saw herself in the glass, the patterned knit cap sprouting strands of dark hair. Her lips were pursed in the quiet of unforgetting.

Why was she never at ease, not since she'd lived with Sorenson, not since she'd left him, the big slobbering klutz? Her picture of him: a round-headed hound chained in his own dark wood, pacing in that dreary place of his imagining. He'd lived in a place of ink, glue, and fame. His work hung in the Courtlaud and the National Gallery. Duped docents proudly described his handiwork as genius. They prattled on about the mythical implications of his compositions.

He had such plans. He carefully accumulated cash. How she sat in the blue chair and mocked him, fanning herself with dollar bills, tucking them into her hair like feathers. She had been proud of him. That made him draw faster and slurp cold coffee, noon to night. But with the night came the drugs and Brett and the dangerous trips to Vienna and Zurich. Luggage left in hotel rooms, train stations, phone boxes, and replicated altarpieces with notched frames. And Brett's "One more run. That'll be it." Always one more run to the coast in rented cars.

Her one more run: Rotterdam, Dover, London, and then home to Aberdeen, this last flight intended to squeeze the fear out of her, estrange grief, cauterize the wound of Sorenson. "A bad plan is better than no plan," Sorenson would say and then crush out a cigarette.

She had to believe that she'd be safe, that she could live quietly. Maybe she could abide as a lecturer for the Open University, once she explained about the money, once McIness knew she hadn't robbed him. It was all just a mistake, a joke of Sorenson's, a prank—gluing the bills to the reverse side of her portrait. She'd return every quid, just give her a chance.

Willem sang "Love me tender."

"I know the words to over a hundred songs," he said. "Try me."

His version of "Knockin' on Heaven's Door" stank, so many accents in the wrong places, but she joined in at the chorus anyway, hoping not to strain her throat or trouble her lungs with too much breath.

Chapter 21

Taylor

At the bottom step of St. Martin's in the Fields, Nichols said, "Stay and give them a hand." He plunged his fists into the pockets of his mackintosh, the only signs of fury, disapproval, and menace that Taylor could see in the man. He expected more from a father for an injured son, a dressing down, chastisement, and teeth grinding.

On the gurney, Evan breathed in spurts, his doe-shaped eyes swollen shut, and his jaw hanging open. Taylor craved to explain, to point out the rips in his uniform, the bruises on his arms and chest, the frightened women, the ninety-nine saved, not the one lost, not the mistake made, not the disgrace. He feared that indisputable data would slip into his personnel file to mark him with its black judgment—promotion denied.

Calls for calm continued over the stage's PA system. Rising mists of tear gas saturated the air. Masked police teams swept into the crowd, establishing control, perimeters, and consequences. Cries and sirens abated.

Taylor watched the emergency vehicles turn toward Westminster. The bare trees on the corner made him feel the cold. He wished for his neat, warm flat, and for all the demonstrators dispersed, safe in their houses. He reentered the church, avoiding Kitner, who was besieged by press and parents at his tiny command table.

The injured clustered in the vestibule, the aisles, and the pews. A doctor sought out the worse of them, touching bloody faces, bleeding arms, swelling fingers. She yelled at Taylor and pointed to medical supplies. He moved with a hitched stride, his hands outstretched for balance. He worked and waited for that umpteenth hour when the doctor or the duty officer would recognize that Taylor limped too much to be of use in a crisis and would send him home.

Home to deal with the flea Nichols put in his ear: find Hines and find out where he'd been, what he'd been doing, and why he happened to be in Harwich the day Glanz met his death. *And don't report until Hines is in custody: another impossible task, another need for a miracle.*

Worry shifted to puzzlement and then to pride. Nichols had instructed *him* to locate and secure Hines. A backhanded compliment perhaps, but a compliment nevertheless.

Chapter 22

Elias

Elias stood at the threshold of Nichols's sitting room. He removed his coat, feeling intrusive, idle, as he heard Lake and Olivar bustling in the unfamiliar kitchen. He recognized the loud thump and clunk of cupboards opening and closing. He'd put out a warrant for Hines's arrest against Nichols's wishes. He might not want a scandal, but Hines had murdered two people, McIness and Glanz.

Elias believed this, and he'd not let Hines get away with that, no matter what that did to the great Metropolitan Police.

Elias turned on the lamp but refused to sit. He drew the curtains, the weight of the cloth a disturbance in his hand. He thought of Evan, his injuries, and his parents' anxiety as they sat in the hospital's waiting room.

He knew too much of hospitals, the long hours in plastic chairs under unpleasant lighting. Hospitals were not places of safety, not places for Evan and his family. Nichols would refuse to leave London, but Jean and their sons must go into hiding, for their sake, for Vernon's sake.

So here in Nichols's house, Elias had gathered Lake and Olivar. Here they'd plan the protective custody of Jean, Evan, and Parry Nichols.

With a click of his heels, Olivar carried in sandwiches, honey, milk, spoons, knives, and serviettes. His handsome coat hung from his shoulders, unbuttoned. Lake followed, gently setting down a painted tea tray on the low table between to wing-backed chairs. The milk in the cream jug didn't slosh nor did the sugar spill from its matching bowl.

Elias sat in a winged back chair. "Lake, you'll take Mrs. Nichols and Parry in your car."

He lifted a sandwich to mouth, realizing how hungry he was, again.

"Mrs. Nichols and Parry, tonight," Lake agreed. He poured tea into Mrs. Nichols's china cups then sat in the other chair, watching as Olivar claimed the ottoman.

"To Conwy. She has family there." The fragrant Earl Grey pleased Elias as he tasted it. His eyelids fluttered as he gazed at their faces. "Not so safe the little town, but she's known there."

He recognized Lake and Olivar's discontent from the rolling of their lips from left to right, their gulping down of disquiet and dissent. He pulled his right hand against his leg, embarrassed that he had been jabbing the air about him as if he held a cane.

"Olivar," he said. "You collect Taylor. He may be back at the station. We three will take Evan to Scotland."

"What's in Scotland that's not here?" Olivar asked then chewed.

"Catholic hospice used for military personnel," Elias said, readying himself for their objections. "It housed half the English poets during World War I. It's not far from

Edinburgh, very safe, with high walls, and a locked gate."

"What's in Edinburgh?" Olivar said. "Or am I not supposed to ask that? More hush-hush British stuff. I get that crap from Nichols."

"It's 'shite' in this country," Lake said, teacup to his lips.

Olivar inched forward. "Is it ever? And what do I need with Taylor? The guy's a wreck. Bum leg, split lip, probably a concussion from the look of him. If you need a bodyguard, get a different guy, one without a 'kick-me' sign on his forehead."

Elias drank the hot tea thick with honey. "He comes with us. If you take turns driving, it won't be a hard trip."

Olivar snatched another sandwich. "Take turns? With this lug maybe, but Taylor?" He elbowed Lake perched beside him on the low sofa. 'You gotta be kidding."

"Taylor." Elias removed his glasses. He tipped his head down and allowed his eyes to dilate, radiating warmth, sincerity, and confidence. This was his plan to ease their fears. "We need Taylor, and he needs protecting."

"What you gonna do with him?" Olivar asked. "Incarcerate him in that old-world hospital of yours or just torture him with Scottish food?"

Elias did not reply.

Olivar and Lake nodded their heads. Eyebrows raised, they slurped tea and bit into sandwiches.

Elias hadn't persuaded them of Taylor's usefulness or the threats to the Nichols. He tried again. "Taylor found McIness. He found Glanz." Elias put down his cup. "If I'd not been sitting opposite at the same table watching him eat a full English breakfast when Glanz was shot, I, myself, would have him in Brixton jail, under guard. He has details of each murder in his head, and we need to keep him alive long enough to get those details onto paper."

Elias's voice had the pitch of foreboding and misgiving. He waited for their contrary response and their pointed displeasure. They chewed.

"He'd need guards in Brixton," Olivar said, the last bit of his sandwich held between his forefinger and thumb. "He attracts trouble."

Elias gave Lake and Olivar their moments of camaraderie and humor. He needed them to work well together. He had much for them to do, and not all of it would be as easy or pleasurable as driving a vehicle through the countryside. He crossed his arms across his chest and brought the conversation back to Taylor. "Now he's allowed Evan to get his jaw cracked open, and we must prevent any further harm to either of them."

Lake stretched. "Evan may have to take some blame for that. His friends got to safety. His girl's gone clean off the planet."

"Knew that one was trouble when we saw her in the Lamb," Olivar said. He ducked to avoid another of Lake's stretches. "So hiding the Nichols family is the plan? Dropping them off at remote hideaways like no one will notice? You thought this through? We're really going to do this?"

Elias smiled. He had captured their attention, and now they would amend his sketch of a plan and make it their own. All would go well.

Chapter 23

Heather

She looked about the smoky Rotterdam train station café, at the travelers seated at tables too small on which to rest their elbows. One fluorescent light flickered near the counter. Others gleamed in plastic holders opposite narrow windows.

She fingered the straps of her rucksack, didn't like it that it stood on the restaurant floor, that she couldn't keep it on, ready to run. She heard remnants of three languages, French, Dutch, and German yet she chose to speak English, low and sweet.

She touched her newly dark hair and laughed. "I never thanked *you.*"

She'd never been a brunette, wanted to stare at herself in every mirror and glass. Disguise—she didn't believe it really worked, but it did delight her and gave her a heightened sense of herself, an excited expectation that at any minute she might be unmasked.

"I never thanked you," Willem said.

He touched his goatee again, laughed in a choking

way, and folded up the rough beige serviette that he'd pulled from the tin dispenser.

More goodbyes, they'd said a hundred, with eyes, with lips, with pats on thighs in speeding traffic. In her head, she urged, all but proclaimed farewell. She wanted to kiss Willem, but he was the wrong man, not Sorenson. She wanted to curl into Willem's lap with her ear pressed to his chest, but it would make them both nervous and draw attention to them. She dipped her head to hide her reddening cheeks and the flash of what couldn't be love. It could only be insecurity. She had to leave Holland. Brett had found her, and he'd find her again. He'd catch her if she didn't go. He'd kill her as he had Sorenson.

She thrust her shoulders back. "You'll meet someone in Spain."

Willem stared through the window at the tracks. "I don't want to keep starting over." He shook his head and clenched his fist. She feared he'd bash the table and make the all-plastic dishware jump. "I don't want to deal with the Bretts of this world," he said, his face scrunched with anger. He shoved the ashtray full of Marlboro butts. "I want my little jazz club and my room upstairs."

"Marta will keep it safe for you," Heather said.

Marta scared the devil out of her, but Heather didn't dare tell Willem, not now, not ever. She'd told Sorenson how she felt about his friends and, a week later, she was looking for a job in Zurich, with "good riddance" echoing in her brain.

Sorenson hadn't had to shout. He'd just ignored her like an ugly lamp he couldn't be bothered to throw out. He'd continued sketching on butcher paper on the flat's uncarpeted floor. She'd gotten the message. She'd taken the train and a bagful of her warmest clothes.

Willem rose as his train was called. He helped her with her pack before shouldering his own bag. They took extra, steadying steps toward the platform as the cross breezes buffeted them.

He helped an older woman with her luggage before boarding and waved from the window as the train departed. Heather lingered by the bookstall before making her way to the ferry. She flipped through *Time Magazine* but didn't see the words, not even the headlines. She pictured Sorenson and knew she must stop dreaming of him, his square face and his rough-knuckled hands stained with dyes and nicotine. How could he draw, hunched, cross-legged on the floor with the desk lamp facing backward? He amazed her. No man had done that before.

Then came the money, lots of it, green bundles, slippery, numerous, delivered by runners, or hidden in art supplies. "Hide it," Sorenson had said to her as it began to mount up, filling drawers. "Take it, bank it, keep it safe. I just piss through money. Tell me when I'm broke, and I'll sell something."

She bought a bigger purse and visited several banks. They'd liked her at banks. They'd smiled as they counted the cash. They'd noticed her gold ring and the tiny diamond and pearl pendant. "Someone loves you," that's what one accommodating clerk said. She kept up appearances after that, pastel suits, matching handbags, broaches, and scarves. No denim, not even the hint of it.

Heather hesitated, ticket in hand. Maybe Willem wasn't as true as he said. Maybe he'd get off at the next stop, phone the police, or phone Brett, and then he'd go back to Amsterdam, to Marta, to his club, to his old life at the cost of a kiss. She'd be in chains within the hour.

No, not Willem. She didn't believe this of him. He kept things simple, made a plan, and he stuck to it. That was how he ran his club and his life. That was how he'd kept Marta all these years.

Willem avoided the wild detours that marked

Sorenson. For Willem, there was no chasing down streets he didn't recognize, no butterfly maneuvers just before the finish line. He eschewed sizzling escapes over low levees and high walls, rejected quick-rich plans and promises. He cooked and played music. That was what he knew. Perhaps Brett knew something else. Perhaps something indebted Willem to him, something that threatened his club or Marta. Now it too late to ask him about it, not that she would.

Fire and burning, that was Sorenson, that was how she still thought of him. The first time he spoke to her, there had come a vision of smoldering ashes flaring to blue flame. It blew through her in the timber of his talk, that crackling American accent. Oh, it fried the gray matter right behind her eyes. The danger of it drew her, dared her, and dashed her plans for a solo existence. Did she pose for Sorenson the next day? Or was it all the same day? Or a month of afternoons with her legs draped across his blue chair in the mess of a room he called a studio? Sorenson scolded as he sketched. "Don't move, don't flex your feet. Serene, think serene, think drapery." Her delusions of selfhood evaporated.

She halted at a tall table, her figure reflected in a glossy poster under glass. Hurrying passengers crisscrossed the train station. She stared at herself, alone and small. Marta's ideas were worthless. This get-up wouldn't fool a five-year-old. Her pack still dwarfed her, and her eyes were as red as if she had, after all, engaged in a tearful, last embrace.

A man bumped her, big, blond, in a stained raincoat, smiling, apologetic. He spoke to her in Dutch. "Did I hurt you? I'm sorry. I didn't see you. I always lose my way in train stations. Okay? You look tired. Such a big pack. Maybe you should sit down."

She smiled and reassured him, no harm done. She

watched him scuttle toward a platform. He wore the polished black shoes of a bureaucrat or an officer of the law and spoke fast like one as well. He carried a small leather satchel instead of the requisite black briefcase.

She wondered if a companion would make her conspicuous. Would the difference in their heights draw attention? Would a man at her side make Brett more or less eager to follow her? And she wanted him to follow her, to England, and into the waiting arms of the police. Then she would be rid of him forever.

She followed the man to the ferry. She'd decided to make use of him. He would guard her and shelter her as only a harried state worker could.

Chapter 24

Taylor

Near the stairs of the National Theatre, between two lampposts, Taylor paused, in a right state over shocking, wretchedly stupid news. Some nutter'd shot John Lennon in New York, shot him dead, for fame, for nothing.

Fifteenth time Taylor had this thought, making him remember the lyrics to "Yesterday," "Help," and his favorite, "Eight Days a Week." He remembered leaning, all rubbery with excitement, over the counter, watching the forty-five spin on the green turntable, the Beatles' voices echoing in the record shop, Raven Records. His heart had fluttered with that desperate, youthful desire to play guitar. He owned an acoustic, standing in the corner near his bed. He didn't play often, the night shift kept him too busy, so he told himself.

Brooding was bad for him he knew. Corrosive, stingy weird pains battered his temples. A bubbling acid stewed in his stomach. Rancor made him ache and made him ignore the strings of white lights reflected in the

Thames, the Christmas bows on low barges and the tiny stars in a heaven big and blameless.

Not easy forgetting. He tried to empty out details from his brain, not like draining crankcase oil. Pull a plug, make a black puddle, and sweep it into the street when finished. Then let rain pound it until it has no color, form, or substance.

Taylor felt substance-less, pounded-upon, being seconded to Nichols without being told about it, expected to drive the commander around the country without knowing where or why.

Meeting people he'd been told not to know. Tossed out of his usual routine and told to plow through piles of receipts and paperwork without meal breaks, assistance, or even a chair to sit upon. And hunt down one of their own, Hines.

Then came the clacking of acrylic wheels on concrete stairs, reverberating shouts, and teenage insults. Taylor smiled at the bumps, thumps, and rattlings. He had no energy to chase the skaters.

"Let them play," he said out loud, not meaning to.

A figure moved too close. He jerked his head toward the stairs.

"Mouse in your pocket, Taylor?" Hines smirked. "Having a chat with your wee imaginary friends?" He smoothed his tie, a minute gesture, careful, superior, like a tongue licking a tongue.

Taylor spun, his chest swelling with intention, with the view of imminent success, and an easy takedown of a bad man.

A grab from behind, his coat forced down over his shoulders, pinning his arms. He heaved himself backward, stomping on a foot. An answering bellow came from Kitner. Wouldn't you know he'd be here? Taylor twisted his head, following the voice. Yellow light flared upon their shoulders as he bent his knees and surveyed the walkway for escape routes: left or right, or over the rail into the drink.

He twisted and tried to free his arms from his sleeves. He couldn't evade the short punches to his stomach. He caved, letting his shoulder drop and edging one arm out of his heavy garment. He kept his body low, hiding his one advantage, his free hand.

"Nichols cast you out?" Kitner asked. "Put you back on the beat?"

Kitner, smiling now, happy as if he were delivering a joke and not a quick blow. Swing, push, and retreat, dancing as he might roughhouse with his mates instead of purposefully beating a fellow officer.

Taylor saw Hines's fat face as a quick left hook connected to Taylor's nose. He sniffed, surprised that it wasn't bleeding. In response, he balled his fist tight and struck out, sliding forward into Hines, a body blow for Hines's crimes. Here it comes, Hines, your just reward: blood for your lip, your nose, your cheek. Taste it, you piece of shite. Taste my fist.

Then Kitner's elbow smashed Taylor's nose, his sight fuzzed but not enough to miss Kitner and Hines as they hauled him toward the archway. Banging, shoving, he judged the strength of the smaller men, heard their heavy exertion and their heavier shoes scrape the pavement.

Taylor jerked his shoulder into Kitner's stomach. Hines kicked Taylor in the shins. He rolled away from the edge, taking Hines down.

"Is this how you killed Glanz? Two against one?"

Kitner pulled Taylor to his knees, both punching. "I didn't kill."

"Shut your mouth." Hines backhanded Taylor. Blood sprayed from his nose. He squirmed in Kitner's grasp, the knees of his trousers ripped on the rough payment as Hines stomped Taylor's legs.

He itched to smack Hines's smooth face to a pulp, but he'd yet to free his other hand from his own coat. Its sodden weight unbalanced him and made him frantic. He head-butted Kitner, but the upward thrust was weak. All he'd done was spark more anger from his two assailants.

But he was wrong. Kitner stumbled and bumped into Hines.

Taylor got his feet underneath him and heaved Kitner to the side. Hines roared and strode forward. He tucked in his elbows, his fists guarding his face.

Taylor snapped his mouth shut to save his teeth. He used the railing to stand, and slid away from the barrier, body and mind set on a crushing revenge.

Hines tripped him. The coat shifted, Taylor let it fall. He blocked Hines's jab but couldn't escape him, so he drove his shoulder into Hines, their breath thinning to strings.

Hines shoved Taylor against the brick wall. "You collected Elias van den Dolder? You know what Nichols calls him? The Prophet?" Hines stepped on Taylor's foot, grinding it with his heel. "You know why he calls him that? Because what he says will happen, happens."

Taylor jumped before Hines could stomp down on his other foot. Hines's lips turned up, taut and white. Taylor felt the man's snorts and the wet air around his words.

Hines gripped Taylor by the collar. "Nichols told you Elias was Dutch Police, did he? See any identification?" His fresh gloat flashed in his face. "He's a captain, all right, Dutch Secret Service. They don't have captains in their police force. They have adjutants and inspectors."

Taylor shook his head. He could outwit them if he couldn't outrun them. He twisted and kicked at Kitner, the weaker of the two. He missed and was startled when

Kitner cried out and held his elbow. Hines's grip loosened as a skateboard hit his head and clunked to the tunnel floor.

A boy in a leather coat and knit cap righted the board, jumped on it, and sped away. Hines swore as another skater rode into him, bashing his upturned face.

"Sorry," a boy in an anorak said to Hines. "Ta." He rode around Taylor, grinning, shouting out his name and rank, before disappearing down the tunnel.

Two more skaters collided with Kitner and Hines, more *sorrys*, more *tas*. Then came a girl in a heavy coat, low on her board, flinging handfuls of sandy dirt. Taylor shoved, twisted, and lurched toward the street entrance, ignoring his bleeding nose, aching ribs, and swelling eye.

Now it was six, seven, against two. The skaters careened, kicking out their boards, delivering their own "up-yours" Christmas cheer. Taylor appreciated their relentless racket beside the lapping river Thames. A foot more, and he'd gain the busy street, traffic, and maybe even people.

He braced himself against a lamppost, sleeve to his nose, still worried, though there was no sign of Kitner or Hines, no shadows in the tunnel. It was bad enough that he didn't know what the whole case was about, and that his mates hated him for leaving Southwark short-handed. And he hadn't had a day off in two weeks. But now his fellow officers bloodied him and left him nearly helpless on a street corner.

He'd never considered leaving the police before, not even when Joan left, when she walked out without so much as a thank you. Dancing with drunks on a Saturday night was one thing, but a pummeling by colleagues? What could he do about it with only kids as witnesses?

The girl helped him stand, smiling as no young teen should smile at a grown man. He saw his reflection in her glistening iris-blue eyes. Boys propelled him forward, draping his coat over his arm. He staggered with the weight of it.

The boys propped him against a phone box, scattering as a taxi driver stopped, jumped from his black vehicle. He yelled at the children, mistaking the boys' aid to Taylor as an assault. The girl looked back.

Taylor accepted the cabby's help, not arguing with him about the skateboarders. The driver remained uneasy and stretched his neck to check on Taylor in the back seat. Taylor kept the driver's handkerchief to his nose streaming blood. His coat lay across his lap for warmth.

At the hospital, an excited young surgeon put three stitches in the cut above his eye, and it did hurt just as the curly-haired doctor said it would, as did the tetanus shot, which Taylor thought was unnecessary, but he couldn't decline.

He didn't comment when the doctor pressed pain medication into his hand. He suppressed a laugh when the doctor instructed him to take the drugs only if he were in pain. He accepted the note that gave him three days off for recovery.

He held an icepack to his face. The bleeding from his nose slowed. His back and neck stiffened. He hobbled down the hallway to use the phone. His resolve to report the assault weakened as he recognized Michael Lake, his baritone voice startling him.

"As I live and breathe, Gareth Taylor." Lake put down the receiver and leaned his left arm on the top of the mounted phone. "You're getting to be a regular Humpty-Dumpty, Taylor, coming here every week."

"I needed another scar," Taylor said. "Symmetry."

Lake looked down the hallway. "Some coincidence you being here. I'm here because two people got shoved off a bus tonight, right round the corner. One's gone to hospital, and one's gone missing. A woman, pretty by all accounts."

"A woman?" Taylor shrugged, winced. He didn't know how long he could stand here talking. He needed to get home. "We get three, four calls a night about women going missing. An epidemic some days."

"This one is the PA." Lake nodded, his voice low. "For that banker you found hanging from Blackfriar's Bridge." He made a swinging motion with his hand and mimicked a death rattle.

Taylor rested against the wall. "Suzanne Cooper." He attempted nonchalance, but he was all-tell: his skin flushing and his lips pinched and dry. He winked as Lake repeated the woman's name.

Lake motioned him to the lounge. "Know how I know?" He held up a small handbag in an evidence pouch. "This dainty landed right under the streetlamp. More coincidence, you think?"

Taylor shifted the icepack to the other side of his face. He gripped the nearest sofa's armrest and dropped onto the worn cloth cushion. He stretched his legs. He wiggled his toes, and none seemed broken. Something to be said for boots. He touched the bandaged over his eye. He wondered if he'd get those three days off given how this murder case dogged him.

Crossing his arms tightly, Lake sat, "Now don't go all quiet on me. I don't like it. So, out with it. How did it happen? And don't give me any bullocks about doors or walls or cupboards."

"Two men," Taylor said. "One held me, one punched."

"Just like that?" Lake asked. "No talking, no fore-play?"

Taylor gripped his ribs as a laugh erupted from his mouth.

Lake allowed his hands to dangle between his legs. "So, who were they? This wasn't a random assault."

"Kitner and Hines." Taylor held his jaw, the moving of his mouth painful. His tongue touched each tooth in turn. He found no holes, no blood, so no visit to the dentist needed. That was a relief.

Lakes stared at his hands. "What'd they want? Or should I say, what'd they'd get?" He looked up and blinked with agitation. "They're a pair of bastards, you know that? They've impeded this investigation, again and again. Even tried to get Olivar sent home. Don't know why Nichols doesn't arrest them both. Now they've done this to you." He swore, took Taylor by the elbow, and examined him closely. "You did get at least one punch in?"

Taylor gripped his jaw again. "More than one."

Lake edged closer and lowered his voice. "Then what?"

Taylor moved the icepack again. "They asked if Nichols was done with me." He tilted his head to stifle a yawn.

"He isn't," Lake said. "Not with Glanz dead."

Taylor straightened and steadied himself against the armrest. "They killed Glanz. Hines," he corrected. "Kitner wasn't at Harwich. I don't think he was involved in that murder."

"So you're a detective now, solving murders? Well done." Lake put a hand on Taylor's shoulder then removed it when it made him grimace. "Don't expect me to be surprised. Olivar's been bending my ear for weeks with their iniquities. But I am sorry you got between their fists."

Taylor guffawed, a sound back in his throat, lips and jaw shut. He repeated the conversation from the tunnel.

Lake nodded. "They planned to leave you for dead,

another victim of the growing crime rate. It's time they got theirs. But I didn't say that, and you didn't hear that."

"They were interrupted," Taylor said. He rocked with pain, patted his jacket pockets for those drugs the doctor gave him. "Kids."

"What kids?" Lake asked. "You got kids?'

Taylor twisted his body seeking an unsore spot. "Skaters. They race about the National Theatre. Sometimes I chase them."

Lake crossed his legs, pondered the ceiling, fingers clenching. "You're a marvel, Taylor. You were rescued by kids you sometimes chase? Hines and Kitner couldn't have liked that."

Taylor flinched. His chest ached so much. He needed a lie-down, but there wasn't room enough with Lake next to him.

Lake examined Taylor's face. "Now don't go all weepy on me. Looks bad. You might have some snaps taken. We can pass them 'round the station. Show the Southwark lads what you get when you're 'seconded to Scotland Yard. Probably stop calling you names."

Taylor scanned for a water cooler and limped to it. "Not likely." He popped the codeine and took a slug of water. "Find Suzanne Cooper."

"Don't tell me my job, Sergeant Taylor." Lake stooped to fill a cup with water. He drank and crumbled the cup with one hand. "I've got enough people doing that already. This Blackfriar's business has paralyzed the Met. It's all top priority and don't ask questions." Lake patted Taylor's arm. "So, what else has Nichols got you doing? We know Hines and Kitner are not after files. They don't clutter their lives with evidence."

"We went to Harwich, but you know that." Taylor dropped his cup into the rubbish bin. "And you're not the only one who's been told not to ask questions." He gripped Lake's elbow. "Find Suzanne Cooper quick, or you might not find her alive. They'll hurt her, if they haven't already."

Lake tapped Taylor hand until he got the hint. "You got it bad, Taylor." Lake shook his head. "She's Olivar's assignment. He'll keep her safe. You'll see her again, if that's what is worrying you."

A woman beloved by a young man, as Taylor himself had been when he had married, even when he divorced. But the marriage ended before the divorce, ended that spring morning when Joan had arrived home in a black mini-dress with gold-streaks in her dark hair and offered neither apology nor explanation.

"You're home early," she'd said, black high heels dangling from one hand. Her small black silk purse was clutched in the other and her lipstick so red and bright upon her smiling mouth. But her smile was not for him.

"You're home late." Taylor'd held the door open as she brushed by him into the hall. He smelled a different perfume, nothing of rose or lilacs that she'd told him she liked.

"Not a crime," she said over her shoulder. "You should know."

"What should I know?"

She hadn't answered. She emptied the wardrobe, the dresser drawers, and the medicine cabinet. She had her mail forwarded to a post box. In the days that followed her perfume dissipated and his notion of himself as a married man fell away. A corrosive pain inserted itself into his eyes, his walk, and his voice for months.

Lake shifted his rugger-body awkwardly in his black coat outlined by the lounge's green leaf wallpaper. His blue eyes softened. He'd heard the melancholy in Taylor's voice. He tried to control the pitch of his speech, but Lake had played him first with sympathy and then with indifference. Taylor admired Lake's skill as an interrogator and wondered what kind of clod of a heart beat in that thick chest.

Lake stuffed his hands into his pockets. "I'll get a constable to run you home. You get yourself assaulted again, you call me straight away. I'll have those murdering bastards meet with some friends of mine."

Taylor parted his swollen lips in the best smile he could manage. "I won't look forward to it." A refrain from a Beatles' tune battered his sluggish brain.

Chapter 25

Elias

A key turned in Nichols's front door's lock. No one was expected at the Nichols's Hampstead home. Lake bolted from the chair and hurried into the hall, Olivar in his wake.

Elias remained seated. He sighed and replaced his glasses on his nose, already wearied by the trip he had yet to take to Edinburgh. He guessed that Jean Nichols hadn't been persuaded to leave England, given Evan's condition and prognosis.

"Elias," Jean called from the hall. Her voice rippled in the air and gave him pleasure. He wanted her to talk to him all night.

"In here, Jean," Elias said loudly.

She bent to kiss him, frowned, and nodded toward Lake and Olivar, hovering in the doorway. She sat down on the ottoman before his chair, her wool skirt swirling about her slender legs. She took his hand in hers, smiling at him. "You waited up."

He was all attention, his fingers tingling. "We hoped

you'd leave from the hospital. Now it seems we'll have to drive you."

"I'll be right outside," Lake said, the hall light rounding him. Olivar didn't speak. His heels squealed as he turned.

Elias patted her hand. "Don't worry about Evan or Vernon. We have them protected."

"As you did today?" Jean asked, her voice barbed. "Did you see him? Half his body bandaged. What happened?" she sobbed, her head on his knee.

"Tonight, you pack a bag for you and Parry," Elias continued in a lecturer's monotone. "Lake will drive you both to Wales. You'll be under surveillance at all times." He touched her hair as if that settled the matter, then bent and kissed her forehead.

"First Vernon sends me from the hospital." Jean raised her head. "Now you want to pack me off like a dog to a kennel? I won't have it." She stood, shoving the ottoman aside.

The light wavered behind her as she moved about the room.

"A banker has stolen money from seven of the richest banks in the world," Elias explained but left out the threats to Nichols and his family.

"And they want their money back." Jean eyed him. "Yes, yes. Vernon told me at the hospital while we waited and waited for the doctor, the surgeon, and the chief administrator. Not that one of them could tell me if Evan will be okay. Okay, that's all I was asking, not an essay on the difficulties to gage head injuries."

"Did Vernon tell you they killed the banker to get it?" Elias stood and padded to her, speaking softly. "They've killed everyone who's had a hand in the fraud or knew of the fraud. So you and Vernon and Parry must go into hiding, for a time, a short time." He folded his hands to indicate finality. "Evan is safe in hospital, and Vernon will see to that. Lake will go with you to Wales. Olivar and Taylor will come with me to Scotland. That makes too many targets in too many places. We'll all be fine."

Jean's eyes widened. "Oh, that poor sergeant. Vernon said he'd been injured." Her voice had the rumble of pity as she placed herself before him.

"He'll recover," Elias said. "Our Gareth Taylor is not toothless, nor small, nor easily captured. But I cannot say the same for you. You must go to Wales." He stopped her and held her by the elbow. "You'll know when to come home. It will all be in the newspapers."

"Papers?" Her body shrank from his, her fists clenching. "What will be in the papers? What you are talking about?"

"Jean, do you want Vernon in hospital like Evan? Or dead?" Elias pulled her closer to him. "Vernon has known the risks for months, since the banks in Italy began to fail. If he can recover sufficient sums of Her Majesty's money, the bank of London will stabilize. But it's still an 'if.' We don't have the account numbers yet."

"Hines." She swore under her breath. "It's his doing, isn't it? I told Vernon so. He wants Vernon's job, and this is how he'll get it."

"Pack." Elias turned her toward the door. "Lots of warm clothes. See your family, enjoy yourself, for Vernon's sake."

"Leave my husband, abandon my son, flee my country, for Vernon's sake?" She paused at the threshold. "How'll that help him?"

He couldn't give her the reassurance she deserved. "You'll have Parry." His eyes flashed as if in REM sleep. "You'll have Wales, waterfalls, green hills, castles, and causeways. People pay thousands of dollars to have all that for a two-week holiday."

"You were a better liar when you were younger." She faced him and held his gaze, scolding him.

He gave her a smile of reassurance, embraced her, and patted her hand. She remained troubled, even as she left the room and prepared to leave her home.

Elias thought her acquiesce too easily acquired. She would do what he asked, but her obedience was a debt. Elias couldn't guess what she might require of him. Yet he would have to obey her when the time came as she had obeyed him.

He went to the hall where a phone sat on a small table. He called the hospital, spoke with Nichols, and arranged for Evan's transport home.

Chapter 26

Heather

She entered the Rotterdam ferry's lounge and claimed a bar stool that faced the windows, giving a wide view of the docked ships. She planned to wait on that barstool until the boarding time: ten-thirty p.m. With luck, that cute, blond man with the shiny shoes would make an appearance to down a last pint before departure.

She pulled a tiny flake of tobacco from her tongue and wondered why Willem removed the filters from cigarettes. His quick kisses upon her lips and face still occupied her thoughts. Safe in Spain wasn't safe at home, her whole argument as they waited for the express train. He didn't buy it. He'd waved her ideas away with big motions.

A seaman slid onto the empty stool beside her. She noticed his blue jumpsuit stamped with the freighter insignia, his clipped blond hair. He was the man from the train station but in different clothes, though same shiny shoes.

She felt flattered, intrigued, and confident in the company of a man who was due on board the very ship she was taking.

"You work on the ferry?" Heather asked. She smiled brightly.

"Purser to the Queen's Star." His English unaccented, he kept his round eyes on her. "Fancy a drink? Karl Heltberg," he said, when she didn't reply.

She laughed as he stuck out his bony hand and introduced himself. "Helen." She couldn't think of anything more original. She waited for him to comment on her yellow eyes and skin. The rest and the drugs had made her stronger but had not cured the jaundice.

He smiled, repeated her name, and looked up at the ceiling. She relaxed enough to drop her rucksack to the floor.

No Brett, no sign of him anywhere. Yet she was certain that he was near. Her disguise wouldn't fool him, no matter what Marta believed. Heather had recognized Brett in his weird getup at the Amsterdam station. She knew him in a minute. It wouldn't take Brett any more time than that to know her in her dyed hair and new boots.

Fear found its way to her brain as they drank dark beer. Karl swilled it with relish as he stared at her face. She kept a pint behind him, holding terror close in, allying with it, forcing a second self to record and analyze the colors of the room: brown and black, hard wood, oak, and ash, the color of the man's hair, eyes, hands.

She focused on the rhythm of noise and voices, watched the drinks, the bottles, and the exits. Two doors led from the bar, but she didn't expect to have to flee. Still, if Brett could trace her though a riot in Zurich and a train station in Amsterdam, he could find her in a seaside pub. He'd bump up against her where she sat. He'd plunge his blade between her ribs, twist it, and draw it out. When she fell from the stool, he'd be a block away with a smile on his face.

Heather's eyes caught the gleam of glasses before the curved backs of seaman and dockworkers. Few women drank here and more than one man, in leaving, gave the purser a pronounced wink. She listened and smiled at her new companion, Karl, who reminded her of no one she knew. That gave her comfort.

He pressed close and spoke of a bunk in his cabin. She might sleep there if she wished. He wouldn't disturb her as he'd be on duty. She thanked him, delighted, as the cold deck was what she'd paid for.

The cabin would have a lock on the door. How else could the purser secure valuables and manifests? What luxury to sleep her way home, arriving rested and dry? And if he wanted favors? She'd wait and see.

Chapter 27

Taylor

Taylor had reported to Southwark after leaving the hospital and was actually given three days leave to recover from his injuries plus the requisite scolding for getting hurt again. Not home an hour before Olivar banged on his door with some orders about Scotland. Another Nichols's outing, and Taylor, at the ready, set out like a packhorse ever separated from its mates.

Separation and loss, lessons they didn't teach in school. Recovery was a subject no one could teach. He'd recovered from all sorts of loss, and it hadn't made him stronger, just scarred.

Now, in the unmarked van, after dinner, but not sleepy, he gripped the plastic passenger seat with one hand, watching Olivar's small fingers on the gear shift. He jabbed in the clutch and swung sharply into traffic. Taylor's feet pumped imaginary pedals, so typical the urge to take control, even when he didn't really want to get to where he was going.

He pressed his right arm against his stomach and

braced himself against the seat cushion, keeping his body upright, smiling at the wreck of his life. This was not a cure for his bruises but caused him less pain when the rattletrap vehicle veered and jerked through the city.

He closed his eyes, letting his ears hear the creaks of the doors and riveted panels. These distracted him from his suffering. He told himself to call his father, to chat up that bird at the cleaners, and to read more. Maybe he should see a play. He thought of Suzanne Cooper that rainy Sunday, fist raised, shoulder-to-shoulder, at Evan's side, behind that cloth banner in Trafalgar Square. He remembered the sight through binoculars, the bright flags, proud banners, and then the surge of panic when the fights began.

"What're you grinning about?" Olivar asked. "It's pitch dark, and we have to drive to some hospital in Scotland in a contraption older than both of us put together."

Taylor shaped an hourglass with his hands. "Suzanne Cooper. Evan's little bird." The lamplight shone gold on the road, and all the other cars spun before his drowsy eyes as whirling tops for his amusement. "She wasn't at the hospital. You'd expect her to be there, wouldn't you? The way she kissed Evan and clung to him at the warehouse." He gripped the seat harder through another curve.

Olivar downshifted through a roundabout. "If she's smart, she's in China. Why? What'd you care?" He didn't look Taylor's way.

Taylor took a gander at the speedometer. "I'd look for her, but I'll be in Scotland for I don't know how long." He touched his chest.

"You want me to find her?" Olivar eyed him, both hands on the wheel. "I found her before. I can find her again. No sweat." As the hub of city traffic eased into a suburb, he said, "You're not having me on? This isn't something Nichols put you up to? He's always putting people up to things. What does he do all day, with all the people he's got doing things for him?"

Taylor shook his head. "She's gone missing. Everyone else who's gone missing has ended up dead. McIness, Glanz."

Olivar punched Taylor hard. "You like her. You dog."

Taylor didn't thank Olivar for another bruise. He felt the flush of heat rise on the back of his neck, the tips of his ears and his cheeks. He strained to keep his lips from rising into a smile, but his skin betrayed him, reddening with embarrassment.

"I'd hit on her, but she'd hit back," Olivar said. "Purse-wielding Harpy. Excuse me for going mythological on you."

Taylor enjoyed the shared thought of a woman in a tight skirt with that tiny black handbag in one hand and her prancing steps in high-heeled boots.

"I found McIness's warehouse, discovered his other life. Big fancy banker hanging out in Fulham selling art reproductions. What a fraud." Olivar tapped the wheel with his left index finger. "The guy owns three houses and doesn't live in any of them. Well, he can't, can he? He's dead." He tipped his head, frowning. "My point is: He's a cheapskate. He crashed with Peter Jurg in a two-room flat next door to his office."

"Maybe he found love," Taylor said.

Olivar slowed the van and rolled to a stop in the Nichols's driveway. "Maybe he found a hidey-hole."

Taylor followed him to Nichols's front door. In a voice almost too slow to follow, Olivar said, "Are you up for this? I mean, no offense, but you look beat."

Taylor gave a hiccup of laughter. He gawked at the little Yank inquiring after his health when everyone else acted as if he deserved any bruising he got.

Olivar knocked, still looking up. "Can't be that funny."

Elias stood there holding a small umbrella, dressed in a thick Irish sweater, black slacks, and a mac. He urged them inside and stood back to let them enter. He pointed upstairs,

"Evan's asleep," he said. "I don't want you to wake him."

Olivar looked angry. His head sank and one nostril flared. His shoulders rose, ready to charge. "And how are we supposed to manage that?" He spoke as if his teeth would break.

Taylor clicked his tongue to wet his lips. "Wake him? Doesn't he know he's traveling tonight?" He listened for voices, running water, or a door slam. The house seemed looming and empty. His body wavered in sympathy.

Elias and Olivar ignored Taylor's question.

"Olivar can slip under the bed." Elias nodded as if that explained all. "You hold him, Taylor." He touched him on the sleeve. "If he wakes." He stopped Olivar speaking by adding, "His medication wears off soon."

Elias pulled a Taser gun from one of the mac's pockets and handed it to Olivar. "Take one shot. Be quick. He'll never know."

Olivar looked at it with crossed eyes. Taylor feared it.

Elias waved them up again. "I'll move the van to the alley."

Olivar gave a nod of acknowledgement. They tiptoed up the stairs, not looking at each other. Taylor kept silent as there'd be time enough on the road to discuss Elias's plan to kidnap Nichols's son, stuff him in a van, and deliver him like a pound of potatoes to a safe house in Scotland.

Olivar slipped into Evan's bedroom and rolled under the bed. Taylor stood at the young man's bedside in the curtained room, the open door behind allowing the hall light to illuminate the sleeping man.

Evan woke and struggled up on one elbow. He pushed the blankets away from his body and groaned low as he reached for a hand-rolled cigarette in the ashtray on the bureau. Bluish smoke encircled Evan's face as his eyes lit on Taylor.

He focused his eyes on Evan, bending toward him, drawing all attention to himself. He took not the slightest glance toward the other side of the bed. So sleepy, Taylor thought, Evan can't even register danger.

Evan's eyes and brow contracted as his back arched with pain. Taylor caught Evan, the soft brown hair trailing over his hands. Sweet smoke wavered as the cigarette fell from Evan's fingers to the floor.

Taylor snapped at Olivar, "That it?" Taylor pulled the prongs from Evan's back, laying the man flat on the bed.

Olivar slipped the gun into a pocket. "Yeah. "He'll be out for a while." He sniffed the smoke, retrieved the cigarette, and snuffed it out. He bagged the butt and rolling papers. He smoothed his coat, and then his hair, turning his head repeatedly, touching all the edges. "What are you, his mother?" he asked as Taylor crossed Evan's hands over his chest and brushed Evan's hair from his face.

"A little kindness won't kill you." Taylor gazed at Evan, wanted to rock the lad to health. "Bloody stupid business."

Olivar peeked through the curtains. "We can take him though the backyard to the van." He took another moment to comb his hair.

"Yeah," Taylor said. "So get the door."

Olivar grabbed a volume from the desk and used it as a doorstop.

They rolled Evan into the bedclothes. Taylor glared at the awkward bundle. This wasn't police work—it was kidnapping, and Nichols and Elias planned it. How was this helping anyone?

Taylor walked with bent knees, trying not to outdistance Olivar. "Damn, he's heavy." He re-gripped his end of the bundle.

All the way down the stairs, Olivar snorted as if he was being kicked in the stomach. They showed Elias their bundle. He surveyed it with a calm face and held a small cloth over Evan's nose and mouth.

"He won't wake," Olivar said.

"We have to be sure," Elias said then led the men across the grassy backyard, opening the gate and then the van doors.

Taylor was surprised to see cots, pillows, and blankets inside the van—actually part of the van—mounted to opposite side, with safety straps and bracings. Why hadn't he noticed them?

He and Olivar heaved Evan into it, his body buoyant in the stringy mechanism. Taylor tucked the bedclothes around Evan. Olivar cinched the safety belts tight and then he collapsed in a heap at Evan's feet.

He tossed Taylor the keys. "You drive. I'll watch him."

"Keep him still," Taylor said. "I don't want Nichols slating us for breaking more of his son's bones. He'll have me guarding dog kennels."

Struggling up, Olivar curled onto an inflated air mattress, which served as the bed of the other litter. "You might live longer." He pulled a blanket from a shelf beneath the contraption. "Close her up, would you? I need my beauty sleep."

Taylor climbed into the driver's seat, noticing a suit-case on the passenger side. Now when did that get there? And what's in it? Was he supposed to bring a change of clothes, extra uniforms? He eyed Elias with more suspi-cion and more distrust.

Elias settled himself in the passenger seat, clicked his seatbelt, and placed his umbrella on top of his suitcase. He unfolded a map with a route highlighted in blue. Tay-lor had expected to drive straight through the Midlands, but Elias's route was via York. Yet another curiosity that he didn't explain.

Misty rain fell. Taylor turned on the radio and fought with the stiff wheel to keep the old machine in a straight line on the slick motorway.

"You know, this is not a punishment," Elias said.

"For me or for him? He belongs in hospital."

Elias gave a loud sigh. "He belongs where it's safe. He will be less of a target in Scotland, and your com-mander will have fewer immediate worries about his fam-ily. We have to give him that if we want to solve McIness's murder."

Taylor didn't ask where *safe* was, not a place on any map he'd never seen. It was certainly not in the back of a rickety van rumbling its way up country in winter.

Miles later, Elias gestured to a lay-by. "You need a rest."

Taylor agreed but was loathe to wake Olivar or Evan. Stretching, worries spun in his head, and he feared that little good could come for any of them from this ramble in the thickening dark.

Chapter 28

Elias

Now that Taylor had changed places with Olivar, Elias closed the back doors of the van. Umbrella held high, Olivar leaned against the engine sipping coffee, the steam of the beverage merging with the young man's breath. The air grew dense about his head.

He crushed the cup after draining it, tossing it in the nearest bin. Still silent, he took his place in the driver's seat, readjusting it, then the mirrors, making no comic slur about Taylor's size and shape. The little eagle, Olivar, narrowed his eyes, bent his head and stretched his neck. He cracked his thumbs and backed out of the parking place.

Elias smoothed the map in his lap. He sensed the other men's unease but couldn't find words to alleviate it. Taylor would obey, his hulking body a weight even to himself but Olivar, he wanted answers, inclusion, a clear plan of right action that would vindicate this late-night expedition and all this secrecy.

"So, after we dump Evan off, then what?" Olivar

asked. He joined the northbound traffic with a groan of gears and tires.

Elias smiled. Only the American had inquired as to Elias's plans. Taylor had not asked a single question.

Elias signaled with an open hand, blinking rapidly behind his glasses. "You will drive the van to London." He inhaled and continued. "Taylor and I will remain in Scotland. A few days only. A visit to Edinburgh castle."

Olivar nodded. "That's what I report?"

Elias tapped the suitcase at his feet. "Report that I'm following a lead. Sorenson restored paintings at Edinburgh Castle and at the University of Aberdeen. I want to see them."

Olivar pointed over his shoulder. "What's he going to be doing?"

Taylor leaned between the seats. "Yes, I'd like to know that."

"Keep quiet," Olivar said. "You'll wake Evan."

Elias tugged at his coat collar. The English air bothered him. "You are both targets. So we, the commander and I, are splitting you up."

Olivar ground the gas pedal. "And the lucky one gets killed?" The vehicle sped up the road, the freezing wind rattled every door and panel.

Elias shivered then reset his face with the grim illusion of patience. "Chelsea Estates Galley distributed more than art. I know you didn't find any evidence at the warehouse. You worked very hard, very thorough, opening crates, photographing works. But the evidence is there, and we, you'll find it. I'm sure of that."

He considered what to say next, what would interest them.

"We didn't find any '*Art*,'" Olivar said. "We found crap. So, where's the real stuff? It's got to be somewhere. Nichols said there was art. I can't go home to San Fran without something to show for my years away."

Elias eyed Taylor. "Slashed. You saw it, at Emile Glanz's cottage."

Taylor stretched between the two seats. "Saw broken frames."

Elias heard groans, twisted to see into the rear of the van.

Olivar turned sideways. "Want me to stop?"

"Check him, Taylor," Elias said. "We shouldn't stop. We're expected. We're to radio in. It's all arranged."

Elias listened while Taylor slid toward the injured man. It seemed a simple plan, transporting Evan to Scotland, but they had no medical supplies. They lacked medical expertise and were relying on a sling, wool blankets, and two small pillows to enable safe transport. Evan swung in his unpadded nest but for how long?

"Sleeping," Taylor whispered.

Elias wiped his glasses and worried about Evan, his friend's son. This trip was meant to save the boy, and it wasn't going badly. There were two men to drive. He could even drive if it came to that. He put on his glasses and peered out the window for a signpost. He expected Taylor and Olivar to remain suspicious right up to the hospital's emergency entrance, the drive with its crushed granite driveway and tall, metal gates, the steep stairs so characteristic of nineteenth century state institutions. Then they'd see the kind doctors, the busy nurses, and the modern treatment rooms. Then they'd be comforted, and Evan would be safe.

At the second rest stop, Taylor bought them coffees and sweet biscuits. Elias poured his into a thermos that he plucked from his valise. Then he crawled into the back to sleep, closed his eyes, and waited for the two men to start talking, his right arm around his suitcase. He hadn't explained to them the danger that surrounded Vernon and his family. How could he tell them that his own knife-wielding son, Brett van den Dolder, had plans to kill Elias and his friends? Elias sent the members of Vernon's family to three different countries. Brett would have to choose a target, and he would be captured or killed by the security forces staking out the family home in Hampstead Heath, the safe house in Wales, and the old hospital in Scotland.

"So what's the plan for me?" Taylor kept his head close to Olivar's. "What am I really doing here?"

"You're *The Third Man*, the one who carried his own coffin." Olivar banged the dashboard. "Damn heater. Ever seen the film? Very British. Everybody cheats each other. Stolen goods, murder, beautiful woman."

Post-war life, Elias thought, they couldn't imagine it—stews without meat, all beetroots and tulip bulbs. His Alise scolded him for stealing from the Yanks, pocketing rolls, pads of butter, honey jars, and silverware. She told him to ask. He would not beg. He'd not fought a war in order to beg.

Taylor sat back. "What happened to *The Third Man*?"

"Gets killed," Olivar said. "Biggest crook of them all. No offense intended. Just how the movie goes."

"I haven't stolen anything since primary school," Taylor said.

"Got caught, didn't you?" Olivar chortled.

"My sister did," Taylor said. "After she stole the radio from me."

"A criminal enterprise." Olivar laughed, tucking his chin into his chest. "That's the oldest family business."

Taylor sipped coffee noisily, as through a straw.

"I'll tell you this," Olivar said. "Police don't like arresting police. They'd rather kill them and squash the scandal."

Elias heard the slap of the windscreen wipers, the rocking of the cot, and Evan's snores. The swaying bed made Elias think of baby Moses in his basket bobbing in the reeds of the Nile.

And she laid it in the reeds by the river's brink.

Both men grew quiet—just the creak of the bucket seat as Taylor squirmed and Olivar worked the clutch.

Elias smelled the rain and the wool of his coat. He took a small vial from his inside pocket. With a penlight clenched between his teeth, he poured the contents under Evan's tongue, pressed Evan's lips closed, and counted to thirty, reciting:

"'And the Lord said, I have surely seen the affliction of
my people, which are in Egypt…'"

Elias watched Evan's Adam's apple and knew that the liquid had been swallowed. Evan would remain asleep. A volcano wouldn't waken him. That was what the chemist promised Elias. He prayed for the recovery of the sick.

"'Is anyone sick among you? Let him bring in the priests
of the Church, and let them pray over him, anointing him
with oil in the name of the Lord.'"

Evan's wounds would heal, but what resentments would dwell within thereafter? Would he look upon his father and mother with apprehension, antagonism? Would he fail to care for Parry? All poor outcomes from this attempt to shelter Evan from further harm, to keep him from the hands of murderers. But what young man would believe an old one?

"You think we're being followed?" Taylor asked, his voice echoing against the window glass.

Elias raised his head in order to hear better.

"On a bum-fuck night like this?" Olivar snorted. "Not a chance."

Elias considered how to quash Taylor's many worries about Hines and Kitner. *I must make a plan*, he thought, *to soothe Taylor and assure the man of his worth*.

"You want me to find Suzanne Cooper?" Olivar asked. "Don't answer. It's all over your face. Relax and enjoy the ride. I'll find her. You keep Elias out of trouble and yourself, too. I'm not driving back up here to drag your sorry ass out of some god-forsaken loch."

Fatigue dulled Elias's hearing. He slept, clutching the blanket in both hands and using the valise for a pillow.

Chapter 29

Heather

In the purser's cabin on the Queen's Star, she sat staring at the washbasin. Twelve hours without Marta's drops and she ached again with that damn fever. Her throat had grown raw from coughing. Her drugs were stowed in some lockbox, evidence Karl claimed. Karl, the alleged purser, the one who chained her to this bed frame. All her sexy moves had been wasted.

"Get some sleep," he'd said. "And the name to add to your prayers, Beers. Aloysius Beers of Her Majesty's secret service."

Then he'd emptied her rucksack. At that little desk, he'd itemized her belongings. He took away her passport, her money, and her knife. He'd given her a receipt on ministry stationary.

She'd held the paper. She'd wanted to shove it down his throat.

Then came the news. "Your friend." Beers'd faced her with his hands on his knees. "Mr. Willem Jurg. Interpol picked him up at the border."

Earlier, she'd awaken at the squeak of the cabin door, rolled unto her side, using her feet to free herself from the bed clothing. She'd watched as first Beers shiny black shoe appeared through the opening. He'd clicked on the light, staring at her before he came near.

He'd smiled, dimples deepening in his ruddy cheeks. "Helen."

She had peered from the bottom bunk, thinking it might be easy to escape from a man with that much honey in his eyes, that much sweetness in his stance. He'd knelt beside the bunk, one hand behind his back, his eyes locked to hers. Up on her elbows, she had readied to strike him if and when he tried to pin her down.

He'd stroked her cheek as if testing for the ripeness of a peach. His lips parted as he drew closer. She'd waited for the caress, her eyes open. His eyes had closed as his mouth wet itself on hers, no extra pressure to part hers. Something had clapped around her left wrist. She'd tugged at the metal cuff repeatedly, swearing and screaming. Her head bumped the bottom of the upper bunk. Another click locked her to the bed frame. She'd lunged at the purser, abusing him in every language that came to mind. She fell from the bed and landed hard on her knees.

He'd stepped to the door and welcomed her to her majesty's custody. "We've a queen, too," he'd said. "Beatrix. We're very proud of her."

"Proud of yourself, you bastard?" she'd yelled.

He'd pushed her back on the bed. She'd kicked at him as he lit a cigarette. "Cigarette?" He'd blocked her punch and pushed her again. "Suit yourself, Heather. The crossing is all night, but then you know that. What you don't know is that we don't provide room service."

He sat at his desk now, out of her reach. He swiveled in his chair back and forth, taunting her. He held up a photocopy of her head and shoulders, a sketch by

Sorenson. She recognized the signature in the right corner. Her mouth trembled with shock. The Dutch police knew her and had been waiting for her. She'd showed her face, and they'd nabbed her.

"We dock in eight hours." Beers told her. "We'll be meeting the London Metropolitan police. They'd like a word with you."

She struggled less. She sat cross-legged and stared at him. She'd cursed him, but that hadn't helped her get out of the cuff.

"Doing my job, as always." He picked his pen up with his left hand. "I've had my coffee, so I guess I'll finish these letters."

She began to plan harm, wrath, and vengeance. She'd wipe that smile off his bland face one way or another. He had to unchain her before they left the cabin and she'd strike him then. He'd be expecting the escape attempt. She would have to be quick.

"I need my clothes." She yanked her cuff. The metal bunk rattled.

"Matron will visit you a half hour before docking." He turned his head and flicked cigarette ash into a plastic tray. He rubbed his eyes with his right wrist, yawning. "She'll help you dress. I'll be just outside."

Chapter 30

Taylor

Taylor braced himself as he felt the van stop abruptly, back up, and rumble down a gravel pathway. He rubbed his right cheek, chilled and flattened from the window. He rolled his shoulders. There wasn't room enough for a good stretch.

Just visible ahead were two gold and black ornate gates with a signboard identifying the hospital. No guard, no bell, no intercom, and no way to warn the staff of their arrival.

"You mind getting the gates, sleepy head?" Olivar asked.

Taylor slid from the seat and pushed the two gates apart. He signed to Olivar who gunned the engine in response. Taylor climbed aboard as the vehicle rumbled up to a startlingly gloomy building with wide steps.

When Olivar stopped the van again, Taylor flung open the back doors and helped a groggy Elias to descend. Evan slept undisturbed.

Three orderlies rushed to them, quarreling. "He

needs a doctor. You're not going to move him, like that?
We can't be responsible."

Two of the orderlies backed away from the vehicle,
ran, shouting toward the clinic's doors for a gurney. The
third Scot with freckled arms dropped them to his side as
Taylor lifted Evan from the cot, cradling him. Snow
drifted from the rooftop, freezing to the edges of the
building, his hair, his jacket, and Evan's inert body.

In the hallway, Olivar unwrapped the bedspread to
reveal Evan in his wrinkled clothes, dirty bandages, and a
jaw slack as if he had died. Flabbergasted doctors and
nurses pushed Taylor away. With increasing anger, they
checked Evan's pulse, breathing and eye movements.
Olivar dusted himself off under the offended gaze of the
clinic's personnel.

Olivar and Taylor submitted to the director's scolding about the patient's condition. Not to mention the
method of transport, their obvious disregard for the
young man's welfare, and the time of day.

"So much for being expected," Olivar said.

Taylor apologized. Olivar followed the gurney down
the dreary hallway—no pictures, no chairs, no plants. A
lemon-scented floor wax grew pungent by heat pumped
through low grates. Elias had mysteriously absented himself.

In a light blue examination room with a single bed
and a white curtain, two nurses, both blondes, changed
Evan's bandages. The nurses glowered as they left the
patient. Taylor put his back to the door. He stomped his
legs to stretch them and to free them of pins and needles.
He waited for Olivar to speak.

"Where'd Elias get to?" Olivar whispered. "I've
worked with him for two years, and he's never been this
cagey." He shifted foot-to-foot, uneasy, his pupils con-
tracting in the brightly lit room. "Somebody's dead or

missing, somebody important. That must be it."

"Emile Glanz." Taylor spoke in that pained way he'd perfected since working with Nichols. "His studio was ransacked, everything smashed. Elias was shocked by it. He collapsed on the doorstep."

"No." Olivar pursed his lips. "Someone closer to the case, to Nichols, to Elias. Maybe somebody from Holland? I need to get back to London now. There has to be a trace, a record, something."

"What do I do?" Taylor heaved his weight against the door as someone tried to open it. "Wait here?"

Olivar sidled forward and exhaled. "You keep close to Elias. Call me if he tells you anything." He spun his watch on his wrist. "Not that I think that he will. But he didn't bring us both up here just to separate us. He's got a plan." Olivar looked at Evan. "A Nichols in every country and guards all around them. Elias will bring them all back together. You can bet on it. It's the why, but the when is what we don't know."

The matron banged on the door and pleaded to be allowed to enter. Olivar nodded, and Taylor stood away for the door. The woman stumbled into the room, gray blankets tumbling from her arms. She and Taylor gathered them as another authority entered with uncompleted forms. In his white coat, white shirt, and tie, the balding man explained that the hospital had stopped handling emergency cases thirty years ago. It had been privatized and now operated as a retreat for those suffering from addictions. The hospital did not operate as a hotel with guests arriving at any hour. Taylor nodded, wondering where Elias had hidden himself.

Olivar left when the third hospital administrator entered to explain policy and procedures regarding admissions. "I hear my mother calling." He jingled the van's keys, smiled, and waved bye.

Elias appeared in the doorway. "You can care for the boy," he said, not raising his voice. "A commander's son. Really, he'll be no trouble. Tell them, Sergeant Taylor."

That was choice, even for Elias. But Taylor described how Evan slept without waking once from London to Scotland, a model patient. Matron and her superiors snarled and rushed from the room to argue about Evan.

Elias lay down on the floor with his scarf for a pillow. "Find a room for us, one with a desk and phone." He closed his eyes, his legs crossed at the ankles.

Restless in a hospital bed of his own, Elias gave out a low rasping groan in his sleep. That noise added to Taylor's other discomforts. The twin bed was too short for him, and he didn't like being with Elias in Scotland, without jurisdiction, without even a change of clothes. But what did it matter what he liked? He'd like to go home. Instead, he waited for Elias to wake, to emit one cross word, one more felonious order, and give him a reason to rise up and hurl a radio or a phone across the room. He'd watch it smack into the wall with great noise and greater pleasure. He'd ended plenty of fights in his time, maybe now was the time to pick one.

Taylor considered his anger, the brimming depth of it. He felt the puzzle of it in his abiding pain, why ribs weren't made of rubber, or, at least, of some substance less fragile than bone. He ached from the rattling drive, from the bruises Kitner and Hines inflicted, and from the slam of bodies in Trafalgar Square. He'd carried Evan, and yet not strained under the boy's weight. Now why was that? Sympathy? Urgency?

Slow healing, that was his lot in these last years. He'd dragged himself from bed to bath, soaking in Epsom salts until the water grew cold. He'd visited the chemist for painkillers, bandages, and heating pads. Then finding when he woke that his shoes were too tight and his belt chafing a gash at his waist until it bled. How many times had he heaved his worn body down the seventeen stairs from his flat to the street, wearing blood as aftershave?

Did that all count as work, as success? Was an inventory of his injuries information to put in an appendix or an epilog to his reports?

He struggled out of his shirt and trousers. He folded them and placed them on the floor. He slipped beneath the bedclothes. He didn't fear for Evan. Taylor knew the boy slept nearby on the ward, so he took this chance to sleep soundly

Waking, Taylor watched Elias alert and happy, bustling as he repacked his belongings. Taylor had nothing to pack, so he dressed and sat on the bed, staring at his shoes.

"Sleep well?" Elias drew the drapes, but little light entered the room. Winter mornings were dark in Scotland. "Carry this for me, please." He pointed to the valise, which stood at the end of his bed.

Taylor took it in one hand and held the door with the other. Elias suddenly sagged as they descended the stairs to the canteen. He leaned heavily on Taylor's arm as if a deathly fatigue had found him out of all the people in the world. Taylor found it a strange show.

"There should be tea," Elias said. "On the sideboard."

So Taylor carried a laden tray to a round table with a noticeably worn cloth. They were eyed by nurses and orderlies. He nodded to them, putting his big, police uniform on view. There followed a racket of little clinks of crockery as personnel piled their trays and left the room.

"We'll go on to Edinburgh Castle," Elias said.

"It'd be closed at this hour, sir." Taylor stared at Elias's trembling hands. "It's half-seven." A bad start to another day.

"Yes, I should think so," Elias said. "But you're a London cop. You knock on the door and see if someone doesn't answer."

Taylor's eyes widened. He clawed the knees of his trousers. His spirits sank deeper. How he longed for the putrid smell of the Thames, the wide-winged flight of the swans, the toot of barge horns, and the safe piles of paperwork that followed an arrest and booking. Ah, for a Southwark shift.

They arrived at the castle more than an hour later, the wretched Edinburgh air biting into them and shriveling Elias to near weightlessness. He clutched Taylor with both hands.

They met an immaculately arrayed duty sergeant. His mistrust drenched them as his eyes roved up and down their wrinkled clothes. He examined Taylor's uniform minutely, looking for errors of detail. He opened Elias's suitcase and pawed through its contents.

"I'll inquire if the commander can see you." His lips sank into a frown, his shoulder stiff with contempt. "Wait here." He exited through a side door with baleful finality.

The guards on duty didn't relax nor turn their heads nor lower their weapons. Taylor glanced about the castle's round courtyard, lit by spotlights and ringed with CTTV cameras. The stamp of feet and the click of rifles seemed to come from everywhere, as if all the dead and buried regiments were rising up to bar their way.

Elias and he remained at the gate until the duty sergeant returned. "The commander will see you." He spoke with barred teeth. "Please leave that here," he said, pointing at the suitcase.

One of the guards took charge of it as the duty officer escorted them to the commander's office, a room wider than it was long, more like a reception room than an office.

Dust-free, it seemed a place to dispense negatives and denials. Florescent lights glowed dull against a false, soundproof ceiling. They wouldn't be staying long.

They faced a slight, bony-faced man with ice-blue eyes, white mustache, and gray hair. He'd been on the phone. The black receiver hung askew in its cradle on a highly polished table with one brass lamp. He shook hands, offered each a seat as the duty sergeant left the room. "Commander Riley Howth. How may I help you?"

Taylor regarded the tall, locked bookcases, the two closed doors, and the two chairs with heart-shaped backs placed evenly before a table upon a burgundy patterned rug. A silver tea set decorated the top of an ornately-carved credenza opposite. The overhead light dimmed the beauty of these furnishings. Taylor hoped they corrected that one day.

A government-issued clock with its round black frame hung over the side door. The minute hand clicked nine-thirteen. Taylor frowned. Discomfort kept him impatient. He knew that there was no hurrying Elias or any of his plans.

"Captain Elias van den Dolder." Elias sat in one of the thin-legged, red, padded chairs. "Sergeant Gareth Taylor." He presented a passport photograph of a young, white male. "You've seen this man?"

Taylor settled on the pink settee to the right of Howth's desk.

"Why, yes." Howth's eyes gleamed through the black-framed glasses he put on. "He did restoration work here, years ago. Is there a problem?"

"Perhaps." Elias produced another picture, a passport photo of a blonde female. "Tell me, was he accompanied by this girl?"

"No, not accompanied. I saw her at the gate some evenings, waiting for him." Howth returned the photos. "He worked quite alone. Actually, no one would work with him. Contentious—"

"He didn't stay at the castle?" Elias interrupted and reached for the photographs.

"No." Howth kept up his indulgent air as he cupped his hands on the desk.

Elias felt the criticism keenly. He nudged his glasses up his nose, a signal of the relevance of the question. "The restoration work was done here then, on site?"

Taylor smelled the lemon tea and desired it. He cocked his head toward Howth and then toward the sideboard. Why didn't Howth offer them any refreshments? The man knew what time it was, and he knew how far they'd traveled.

"Of course." Howth's voice had that pitch of dispute. "Nothing leaves the castle, Scottish property. The restoration area is in the basement. Shall I show you?"

"Perhaps later," Elias said. "Do you recall which paintings he restored? It would help us to see them."

Elias said *us*. Us meant take notes, forget nothing, and keep alert. Taylor wrote in his notebook. His stomach growled low, and he grew thirsty.

"This way." Howth rose slowly from his chair and pointed them toward the side door. "They hang in the foyer of the main entrance." Howth led them to the main gallery. "These two portraits, lairds in the service of James the Fifth. Heavy lacquer had made them very dark. Our Scottish heritage, you must understand, is very important to us. These portraits have a number of symbolic details, which were obscured by dirt. You see them now."

Elias nodded, impressed. "And you photographed each of your works at monthly intervals, for insurance purposes?"

"Of course. We keep a very strict accounting of the art work and jewels here at the castle." Howth snapped out the last words, offended. Elias bowed, chastised. "What's this all about?" Howth asked, blinking. He stood back from the portraits.

"Fraud," Elias said. "Works that Mr. Sorenson restored have been revealed as copies. The originals' locations are unknown. So we came to see these."

"You're saying..." Howth spoke to the portraits, seething.

"You might need to reestablish their authenticity," Elias suggested, his voice stronger.

Taylor waited for the rush of orders that did not come. Howth remained transfixed before the portraits.

Elias poked Taylor toward the exit sign. They said their goodbyes, but Howth didn't answer. The duty sergeant found them near the castle doors, returned Elias's valise, and exhibited happiness at their departure. Rain pelted them. They huddled against each other as they crossed the courtyard and hurried from the castle.

A waiting taxi took them to the Bedford Hotel and, surprise, they had a reservation. Taylor took the room key, rode the lift with Elias, and counted to ten under his breath. He didn't ask what came next.

Chapter 31

Elias

Stepping away from the Bedford Hotel's front desk, Elias allowed a bellhop to take his suitcase. Inside their room, he phoned Nichols as Taylor stretched out on one of the beds and fell asleep. The tasteful bedclothes were wasted on him in his fatigue.

"Evan is safe. He won't be found, but he'll need months of therapy." Elias shifted the receiver to his left ear, sitting in the thin-legged chair at the writing desk. "The doctors were not prepared for so many injuries, Vernon." He pursed his lips as Nichols complained. "Of course, they promised a full recovery. What else would they promise?" He twisted the cord and surveyed the ceiling. One foot tapped. "But Evan will be the deciding factor, you know that." He stood and shuffled left and right on the tawny carpet. "Give him a chance, Vernon. Let us see what he's made of. Let's focus on the investigation. Has Olivar arrived yet? No? Let's talk again when he has. Yes, goodbye."

Hanging up the phone, he sat again, watching Taylor

sleep. He looked at his watch, giving the man an hour to rest and himself the time to dress, order a meal for them both, and plan the rest of the day.

Repeated raps on the door roused Taylor. He pushed himself, spider-like, to his feet as the door opened. He reached for the desk lamp, his eyes blinking too rapidly for actual focus.

"Just over there, please." Elias directed an obliging waiter to place a covered tray on the small table by the window. He tightened his blue dressing gown, self-conscious that his hair was wet and his feet bare.

Taylor sank back on the bed, his arms out-stretched. The pillows bounced. Elias smiled as he lifted the plated cover and Taylor heaved himself upright, sniffing the full breakfasts decorating the table. In seconds, he was seated, crunching toast and jam, wiping his mouth with the little serviette the Bedford Hotel provided all its guests.

Elias sat and reached out a palm to the coffee pot. He didn't say that he'd paid extra for the eggs and bacon so late in the day. But neither had had enough food at the hospital and nothing at the castle.

He moved with less stiffness, having conned the management to turn up the heat—hardly a sauna, but warmer than either the van or hospital. He lifted his cup. "I'll be putting in another call to Vernon. Do you wish to speak to him? Give him an update?"

Taylor speared a pair of rashers. "No."

He chewed intently. His body rocked with a motion, suggesting anger or anxiety. Elias struggled with the assessment, judging he had better prepare for an upheaval.

Laying aside his silverware, Taylor excused himself. Yawning, he stripped down to his underclothes and socks. Before turning back toward the bed, he piled his clothes by the door where Elias's own clothes waited to be cleaned and pressed.

"Rest," Elias urged. "We've nothing to do until Vernon calls."

Elias drank coffee until Taylor snored. Then he called Nichols, speaking more softly than normal. "Taylor sleeps. He's been very helpful. But as to the other matter at the castle, Captain Howth, hasn't initiated any action. I can't say what he'll do." He held the phone away from his ear. Vernon all but yelled. "Vernon, if the works are fakes, his career is finished. Do you expect him to risk his reputation on my say so?" He shifted the phone again and rubbed his left ear. "He'll take it slow if he ever initiates an inquiry. We can't count on his assistance. We'll have to locate other works Sorenson restored. Wait. I hear something."

He heard footsteps outside the door, the jingling of keys and also the heat puffing through the grates. He held the receiver to his chest, muffling Vernon's voice. He slid from the chair, trying to see under the door. But he could see nothing but carpet.

No one tried the handle, and he relaxed. "So, what of the girl?" he asked. He tapped his knee with his fingers, but his arthritis was impervious to self-massage. He would be even stiffer in the morning, and that would trouble Taylor. "Which one? Damn you, you know which one: Heather."

Taylor turned over in the bed with a great creaking of wood. The bedclothes fluffed and ruffled about him.

Elias stood and looked at him before settling back in his chair. He lowered his voice. "Beers was tracking her. Hasn't he called you?" He cupped the receiver against his shoulder and rubbed his eyes. "Yes, we—Taylor and I—will visit Stirling and then Aberdeen. We'll collect what evidence we can and return. Has Olivar arrived? Not yet? Wonder what's taking him so long?"

He let Vernon have the last word. Silence and disappointment followed their disconnection. Vernon would not act. He should order the arrests and end this threat to his family. What was he waiting for? Exile, banishment, was that what he wanted for Jean and Parry?

Elias lifted his left leg, his hand under the thigh. The stretch did not relieve the pain. Arthritis dealt a creeping death. It cut into speed, balance, and confidence. It bored into joints and left the bones raw, as fear did to the mind, as inaction did to the soul.

He dragged the chair to the radiator, hoping to warm himself completely. He wondered how he'd ever sleep, searching his memory for a prayer for warming the soul. He pulled the duvet from the bed, wrapped it around himself, settled in the chair, and slept much later then he intended.

∽∾∽

The dusty smell of burning made Elias jump, his cocoon inhibiting his progress. He slid his glasses up, glad he'd forgotten to turn off the desk lamp. He saw no fire and no smoke and then asked himself what woke him. He sniffed loudly as he replaced the duvet on the bed. He turned on the bedside lamp and looked at his watch. Four hours had passed while they slept. He moved the curtain and stared at the darkness blotting out the rain. He rested against the bed frame, unease making his hands and feet tingle.

He stared at the white radiator. It had no glow. It couldn't be the source of the burning. He padded about the room and touched the walls, doors, and light switches. He found no hidden heat, no soft places, and concluded nothing. He decided not to repeat his efforts. He opened the door and stared at the carpet lining the hallway. It was wet in spots but none outside his door. He examined the door lock and the hinges for scratches. He saw none, but that didn't comfort him at all. A voice behind him set his legs quivering.

"Housekeeping," a female voice said.

Elias waved the woman into the room and pointed to the pile on the floor.

He smiled at the woman. "Cleaned and pressed, please."

She smiled back, bending to stuff the clothes into a linen bag.

He decided to rest again. This was no day to be traipsing about outdoors. He quaked at every sound. What was wrong with him?

He woke again, but Taylor did not. Elias phoned the concierge, ordered dinner—a chicken with potatoes and peas. "Yes, wine, some soft rolls, butter, and gravy."

He wanted more heat. He couldn't order that from the restaurant. He did order clothing for Taylor as well as toiletries for the young man.

With a rustling, Taylor woke. "Good morning," he muttered, his voice sluggish on his scabbed lips. "Is it morning?"

"Not quite." Elias sat at the small table again, heaped with covered dishes. He held up a bottle of Pinot Noir. "Suppertime. Will you join me?"

Taylor rose with a toss of the duvet. He stepped to the window and heaved the drapes apart. Street lamps blazed into the room. Their yellow light silhouetted him as he stood there bare-footed.

"Your clothes have been cleaned and returned," Elias said.

Taylor walked to the chair where his uniform hung, wrapped in plastic. Two new shirts, a pair of jeans, underclothes, and socks were stacked on the table. He lifted each, confused at first. Beside them lay a brown paper package with a chemist's logo.

"I thought you might want to clean your teeth," Elias said.

Taylor thanked him and carried the lot into the washroom.

Elias wondered if he should call Vernon again while Taylor was busy in the shower and wouldn't overhear their exchange. Vernon would want an update, no matter the time of day. Elias refilled his glass, moved to the bed, and dialed.

"Cold," he answered to Vernon's inquiry after his health. "Any calls from Edinburgh Castle? We could make a second visit."

Without X-rays of the Scottish portraits, Elias wouldn't be able to identify the works as copies and threaten Sir Howth's stewardship of Edinburgh Castle. Vernon knew this, but he didn't want Scottish authorities to challenge Scotland Yard or to demand a voice in the inquiries. Elias had to let the matter drop.

"We'll proceed to Stirling tomorrow," Elias said.

Nichols agreed as the water in the bathroom stopped. They disconnected with still so much unresolved. Elias returned to his chair and ate. Taylor joined him, clothed, hair wet and his face red with bruises. He ate happily as Elias detailed the next day's plans.

ℰᕐℰᕐᕱ

At the train station, Elias purchased first class day passes, sending Taylor to buy the day's newspapers. He didn't expect any news about their case, but there might be some tidbit about which they could talk. He wanted Taylor to talk, to be the fount of comfort and reassurance that Beers was, but Taylor kept mute, as much company as a blank book. They remained as if strangers en route, eyes busy, mouths shut. Elias read *The Guardian.* Taylor read *The Scottish Times.*

Red chimneys popped into view between trees and high hedges as the train made its elevated way west from Edinburgh. The mist turned to rain. The carriage windows fogged and chilled Elias's face. The wood seats shook with the elevated train's movements, but that noise didn't muffle the crinkle of the newspapers as Taylor read his own paper and then Elias's. That sound absorbed Elias as it was so reminiscent of every lazy Sunday morning. He thought, when he returned home, he might get a dog to have a new sound in the house. He took a small black book from his coat pocket and studied each page intensely.

At Stirling castle, Taylor held the umbrella over Elias's head. It sheltered them little. Their clothes were whipped by the cold wind and rain.

Elias examined the ponderous, odd statuary in the castle's courtyard. He compared it to the sketch in Sorenson's black book, and stared at the fountain through his glasses, his head jutting forward.

Taylor looked down at the page then gazed up at the ramparts and archways. "That's very good."

"Yes, it is." Elias turned the page. "See the uneven stone and the broken faces. Sorenson, he captured those perfectly."

Taylor regarded the bulbous fountain, its thick base, upward straining. "I'd never have noticed that."

Elias closed the book. "Talented. A loss. You can look if you like."

"We should get out of this rain," Taylor said.

Elias bent against the increasingly sharp air. "And there's more: villages, highland plants, cows, coastlines of Aberdeen. What would attract a restorer to the coast of

Aberdeen, do you think? We'll go there tomorrow. See what he saw. He sketched wherever he went, always details: hands, bricks, gratings, fountains, lamps, the girl—his muse."

He walked carefully along the slippery walkway. Taylor followed, measuring his stride to keep the umbrella over Elias's head. Taylor stopped and examined the muddy ground which was liquefying before his eyes.

Elias craned his neck and counted the cars in the carpark. Taylor counted too as the quiet disturbed them. Scanning the distance, they listened for snaps, breaks and rustlings.

No threat appeared. Few people came; fewer remained outside in the shelterless ruins. Taylor's upraised arm trembled with the continued effort of sheltering Elias from the pelting rain.

Elias pitied the young man who hovered. He turned his head, his hair blazed with wetness. "You're cold. Wet through, surely."

Taylor allowed himself a shiver. "Yes, sir."

In the puddles, the turrets of Stirling Castle shimmered.

"Yes, well, perhaps we have seen all there is to see. A drink, sergeant?" Elias asked. "I could use a drink."

Taylor looked in Elias's face. "Conductor said Lord Darnley's offers a nice lunch. Not far from here."

Elias reached for the umbrella and nudged Taylor forward. "We can tell him how we liked it on our return trip."

Taylor braved a suggestion. "I'll find a taxi, shall I?"

"Yes, please," Elias said as Taylor walked through the car park and banged on a taxi driver's window.

"Lord Darnley's." Taylor pointed back toward Elias.

The driver nodded and waited for Elias. In a few minutes, they sat at a small table with a tiny window at their back. The small café sported dainty tables, chairs, lamps, as well as linen tablecloths. The potpourri marked it as a place for trysts. Even seated, they looked out of place.

Elias drank a beer. In this cold place, he perspired, twisting in his seat, glancing at the front door. He felt sure that they had been followed.

Taylor noticed. "Expecting someone?" He sipped the local ale appreciatively.

Elias set down his glass. "Not expecting," he said. "But I heard an odd scraping sound at the fountain. Something dragging. Metal, maybe wheels. You didn't hear it?"

Taylor raised his eyebrows. "With all the noise of that rain?"

"I'm old but not deaf," Elias said. His face grew bright with hidden knowledge, smug certainty. He had Taylor's interest now.

Taylor bristled as the rain pounded on the roof and the wind wailed through the doorframe. The umbrella hadn't kept him dry, even with his overcoat buttoned. Would more rain really hurt him? "Would you like me to check outside?"

"No, Sergeant, don't bother."

Elias beamed as the coffee was set upon the table with cream and sugar. He was sure Taylor would talk all the way back to the hotel. "I need to rest," he said. "Tomorrow, we'll visit Aberdeen."

Taylor added sugar to his coffee. "I'll phone the commander."

Elias gave a contented click of his teeth. "You do that."

Chapter 32

Heather

Chained in this too-clean, little cabin of the Rotter-dam-Dover ferry, she knew the sea swelled all around her, but she couldn't feel it. She cursed Beers for tricking her, for taking her shoes and her back-pack, for leaving her hungry, humiliated, and hurting. He'd taste hell. She'd make sure of that.

"Sleep," he'd said. "It'll do you good."

She didn't want to do *good*. She wanted out of here, away from the two closed cupboards, the three locked desk drawers, and that armless, metal chair. She stretched a second time, bracing one foot against the desk. With her free hand, she patted its surfaces but found nothing that might dig or pry, or function as a tool. Why was there no paperclip or pen cap handy?

"All the years of carrying a Swiss army knife *just in case*," she said.

Here was the case and where was her knife? In a chest, inside a locker, on another level of the ship, and that hateful purser had the only key. All smirk, he slunk out the door, one last whiff of Dove soap marking his wake. He was another proud strutter like Sorenson, not like Willem.

She knew Willem wouldn't sell her out, even if he were in police custody. She hoped the purser had lied, hoped that Willem caught his train and that he'd have some peaceful days in the Spanish sun. If she'd gone with him, would she be there now? Would she be safe on a quiet shore, a glass of a rioja in her hand, Willem speaking of music, she nodding with the burn of loneliness gone from her mouth? Both of them bathed in a healing steam of his talk, his nearness, and his commercial opportunism. Or would they both be jailed, side-by-side, in an ancient and foul Madrid cell?

The handcuff slid up and down on the bunk frame, scraping her wrist raw. Her free hand swept the air. Still, she couldn't reach the door or the porthole. She needed something heavy to smash their latches. Examining the bed, which was bolted to the floor, she flipped the thin mattress with some expectation. Then she dropped it and sat on the floor. The bed's notched wood slats wouldn't do. She was here until they let her go, which they wouldn't. They had a plan for her, and she was not going to like it.

Her cough seared her throat. She spit yellow goo in the waste bin. She needed medicine, but there was no one to ask. The purser wouldn't help her. He took pleasure in chaining her. He'd get his. She had a plan, too, and it involved a few sharp slaps to that purser's shiny face.

The metal edges of the cabin caused her to think of Willem's club, of the steel frame on the silver mirror over his bar, the aluminum shakers, and the shiny shelves that held the spirits, whisky, vodka, rum, and gin. She remembered the dimness of the bar and recalled that strange afternoon.

Her eyes took a while to adjust to the darkness and Sorenson didn't help any, bumping her and nudging her forward. Not a patient man, Sorenson reeked of willfulness. She hadn't thought of that at the time. Then her eyes had fixed on Willem pinned to the bar by Brett's elbow, Brett's arm crushing Willem's Adam's apple. She'd seen blood at Willem's earlobe and a knife cutting. How gleefully Brett flicked it through Willem's hair and Willem's foot slapped the old linoleum, his only expression of fear.

They intervened, not a single word said by either of them. Sorenson had pushed her, and she shoved stools out of the way. He had grabbed Brett by the shoulders and slammed his head into the wall. She'd heard this as she wrenched Willem from Brett's grasp. She'd gripped him around the waist, draping his arm across her shoulder. Blood had dripped down Willem's neck. His fingers were so wet with it that she feared he wouldn't make it.

The knife had clattered to the floor. She'd kicked it toward the door.

With Sorenson, she'd hauled Willem into the nearest shop, calling out in English that their friend had been stabbed. No, they didn't recognize the assailant, just some punk in a denim jacket and tight black jeans. Then the shopkeeper had recognized Willem and phoned for an ambulance. The assistant had brought a medical kit and tried to stop the bleeding with gauze pads.

The three of them had waited in the shop and then in the hospital, keeping silent and circumspect and never hinting at the real events. They believed Brett was half way to Austria as Willem was patched up and warned about secondary infections and tetanus. Sorenson had kept squeezing her hand as he smoked with deliberate exhalations.

She had felt proud of Sorenson, for his Yank sense of

justice and for his damnable willingness to interfere. He could be such a big-muscled goof. Heather missed Sorenson. He could have gotten her out of this.

Chapter 33

Taylor

In the warmth of their room at the Bedford, he sat by
the draped window. The desk lamp illuminated
Sorenson's sketchbook. Elias slept as the night
waned. Taylor sipped his pint of beer, wished he could
talk to Olivar or any of his mates at Southwark. Some one
of them would tell him a joke and change his black mood.

He began to recognize the various mediums—
charcoal, pencil, ink—used in the dated drawings. He
liked the portraits and stared at them. One face seized
him: Heather. Even if he'd not been told, he'd have
known she was British, with that fierce, sometimes sour,
"piss off!" look in her eye. He gazed at the arch of the
lean neck as she turned her head toward the viewer. Her
aggression captured in those unsmiling lips, spiky hair,
and arched breasts with arrow-sharp nipples.

Even when the sketch consists of only her head and
shoulders, he felt the wholeness of her body. He wanted
the weight and shape against him. Warm and white. he
desired to stroke that small round face and kiss that up-

turned chin, those breasts, the curve of that spine, then thrust into her hard. Sorenson had sketched her to keep her near him, keep her coming back to him. Taylor understood that and felt it strongly. There was pleasure and command in those drawings, a desire satisfied utterly.

He hadn't even met her, and he already feared for her. Interpol, Scotland Yard, FBI, and who knows who else, they stalked her. And he and Elias, they waited in this Highland town for the announcement of her death. They'd be on scene when the matron presented herself at the family door in Aberdeen.

"Mrs. Hiscocks, accept our sincerest sympathy for your loss."

They would hear the bad news. They'd watch as the mother collapsed in the policewoman's arms, on the sitting room floor, the newspaper unread and the tea going cold in the pot.

And Suzanne Cooper? Had the knock already come to her parents' door? The funeral notice read out at Evensong?

Taylor finished his beer, but his thirst continued. Frost and sleet had scraped his throat raw. He swallowed with pain and gulped grief.

The whole of the next day, their third day in Scotland, he shivered, holding the umbrella aloft while Elias stared at the rockiest coast they'd ever seen. His new jeans hung heavy with dew, his trainers squished and slid in the mud.

He'd wearied of Elias's company. They had ceased to be acquaintances but had not become friends.

Dangers abounded. Sea air burned their lips and the stirred spray iced their hair and faces, at least Taylor's, though he saw Elias wipe his own cheeks with his sleeve. White-topped waves splashed against the Aberdeen palisades and jutting rocks.

They stood so close to the edge that either could have pushed the other in and called it an accident.

Taylor stepped carefully about on the thick grass. The cattle didn't approach them but huddled, heads down, near a wood fence. He smelled the cows as they turned from the sea. Rain leaked into his shoes. He hoped they could be saved.

The umbrella snapped, its prongs bent as a slicing gust ripped it from his fist. Elias gripped Taylor's arm. They tottered in the muddy ground, the wind blistering their faces. Elias called him Sergeant as if he wanted for a name, as if Captain Van den Dolder, if you please, suddenly did not know him from an alley cat.

"You think Sorenson brought her out here?" Taylor asked.

Elias's breath puffed visibly. "I think she brought him. And more than one time, different dates, you saw them, plus the weeks of restoration."

Taylor stomped side to side, his clothes wet through. "There's no place for a landing. No beach, no dock, no jetty."

Elias pointed out toward the foggy horizon. "Ship to ship. A sloop, maybe a speed boat. It could be done, like a rescue."

Taylor backed away from the cliff's edge. "In these seas? Aren't they patrolled?" He felt the isolation of the spot. Any scream might disturb the cattle, but the noise would never bring help.

Elias looked where the rocks were sharpest. "Yes, by Her Majesty's Service." He bowed his head, wiped raindrops from his glasses.

Taylor wondered if the old officer might be ill again. Elias straightened as if he'd been called. Taylor heard only the noise of the sea and the belled cattle.

Elias pointed to the building behind them "And that

farmhouse, he sketched that. Heather's family owns it. It's been under surveillance for weeks but with no results. No one's come back to it. Perfect cover."

Taylor stared, shifting left and right. His brain buzzed with the possibility of being shot for this place reeked of threats. "Cover?"

"For a drug mule. White powder among art supplies. That's what we found in Sorenson's flat." Elias made a triangle with his fingers. "Zurich, Amsterdam, Aberdeen. Olivar knows, Nichols too."

Taylor shuffled. The slick grass clung to his shoes and trouser legs.

He wanted to be indoors. Lea, meadow, copse, and dale—none of these had any meaning to him, being urban, London-born and bred. Road, walk, café, and pub constituted his woodland haunts.

"He knows? Then what are we up here for?"

"We bring him proof," Elias said. "Your commander won't act without proof, so he says." He climbed up and over the cattle gate, stepped down into the narrow road that led to the farmhouse. "Then he'll be made to resign. He doesn't want to resign, stubborn man. Not like me, I am counting the days. You probably don't count days."

Taylor stamped some grass free and changed the topic. "What can we prove by being here?" Talking made his chapped cheeks and lips sting.

Elias bent into the wind, evidently in pain. "We capture that someone who's watching us. You understand? We're being followed, and they're being followed. They run for cover, and we catch them."

Taylor shook with the cold, and, now danger: his unprotected head and his unarmored body. "We stay out here all day?"

"No, Sergeant. I am tired, just as you see." Elias released his hands. "Back to the city, I think. I'll rest at the hotel before dinner. Call the commander while I sleep. He'll be anxious to hear from you."

Rainwater showered over the eaves of the farmhouse and pooled at their feet, It splashed and soaked their shoes and trousers. A police vehicle screeched to a stop before them, scattering the gravel coating the mud driveway. The driver invited them inside with a honk of the horn. Taylor helped Elias into the panda car, hoping they'd soon be back at their hotel.

He didn't see whoever drove the cattle from the barn, but he didn't believe that the beasts went willingly into that cold field.

He tucked his head, as much for the lowness of the roof as for his expectation of harm. The cops laughed, sped off, racing into the storm.

Chapter 34

Elias

As the police car sped away from the farmhouse and the Aberdeen coast, Elias stared at his hands. The cold here had an unfamiliar smell, a tinge of granite instead of sea, as if he stood at the bottom of a well. Scotland didn't suit him, so tiring, harsh, and primeval. The towns seemed cramped, the hills empty. Here were places of hidden crimes, secret societies, and warrens of ritualized disparities. He couldn't get away too soon. He wanted to hear no more of highlands and lowlands and kingless wildernesses.

Why was there no moon? How did one mark night and day without a sky overhead? Clouds and storms and misty fogs masked the heavens. In Gaelic, no doubt, there were ten words for each. In Dutch, there was but one: *slecht*, bad.

In the hotel, he found worse. The bedclothes had been ripped from the bed and all the sheets torn. Slashed into strips, the drapes dangled from their rods. Slivers of white glass stuck into the carpet before the washroom door against which they had been dashed. The two chairs had their seats gouged and legs broken. Even the handsome table lamps were irreparably damaged.

He pushed Taylor inside and slammed the door. Neither spoke. The ruined furnishings seized all their attention. They stood stupefied by destruction and the havoc that was revenge. The ugly mess that said they would be next to feel a blade deep in their guts.

Elias moved to the middle of the room. He and Taylor must make a plan against this outrage. They must stand guard. Brett waited beyond that door, idling, fingering his knife. That man wanted to hear their cries of terror. He thrived on others' anguish, fear, and misery. He watched for Taylor to bolt from the room, red-faced, mindless with anger, leaving Elias unprotected. Then Brett would strike.

Taylor held the ripped bits of his uniform. There wasn't one seam intact, not cloth enough to make a collar or a cuff.

"Let Vernon pay for that," Elias said. "He owes you that much." He removed his raincoat and let it fall upon the bed, as yet unbroken. Should he tell Taylor of the danger without? Would he seek it? This he must not do. Brett would cut Taylor's throat and then Elias's.

Taylor's great green eyes stared fixedly at him.

Elias sank onto the exposed mattress. His heart beat frighteningly. He couldn't calm himself. His feet were weights in his shoes and his hands rocks in his gloves. Protection, where could they find it? Not behind a locked door or a keep. They were floating-targets, as Olivar would say.

Taylor raised his great arms and jammed the scraps of clothing into the waste bin. The tin pail popped with the force of his fist. He slammed the wardrobe doors twice. Then he tore the curtains from the rods and heaped them on the mound of bedclothes. Unexpectedly, he threw open the window and allowed the rain to add to the ruin.

Elias wanted him to close the window and stop the cold. It stung and bruised him. Instead, he let Taylor stew. Reaching for the phone Elias found that it, too, was in pieces. He'd have to risk a trip to the front desk, alert the management to the wreck of their room, and the possibility of a killer loose in the hotel.

"I'll speak to the manager," he said. "We'll need a change of rooms."

Taylor came out of his stupor. He closed the window and sat on the floor.

Elias scuttled through the door and down the steps to the front desk. The manager apologized and offered them every amenity. Elias thanked him and explained that a plane would take them back to London, home by bedtime. The local constabulary would conduct the investigation and write a report for the hotel's insurance company. The manager must find them another room and keep locked the room they were vacating.

Taylor assisted the local cops as they searched room by room. Elias felt Taylor's inattention to him. He knew that Taylor was lost to him. Taylor would never bring him sweet coffee like Beers did or walk him home when the weather was nice. Taylor brimmed with righteous anger and might well toss Elias from the plane's emergency exit the moment they were airborne. An exaggeration, of course. Less was to be feared from Taylor than from the manager of the hotel. But Elias wanted more from Taylor than from any concierge or clerk. He wanted to be brothers-in-arms.

Chapter 35

Heather

The Rotterdam Ferry bellowed its approach to land, waking her. This wasn't the first disruption to her sleep since the evil purser left her. She'd started twice from dreams of red dresses, tree houses, rope ladders, and secret entrances. Her unconscious mind never let up. It tormented her with images of getting in and getting out. The urgency remained in her body. She was a message that had to be delivered against all odds.

That damn infection burned her as well. She crouched and held onto the bed as the wracking shook her. She needed Marta's drops, but she knew she'd never see them again. They weren't in her future any more than a walk by the Serpentine. She laughed at her own little joke. There'd be no joy this morning, just a short walk followed by a long incarceration. For forgery? Money laundering? Theft? All three? What evidence did they have with Sorenson dead?

She decided to let *Them*, big *Them*, inform her. Maybe she'd meet some MI-6 types, all Eton ties and private incomes. Maybe she'd get a deal: "Where's the art, girlie? Tell us, and we'll let you live out your days in Tasmania, an island we control."

She jerked her own chain, not for the first time. She closed her eyes as her head drooped. She let the fever take her back to those imaginary houses with wobbly stairs and locked windows. She'd wear that red flag of a dress and claw herself a hole to infinity.

Chapter 36

Taylor

The Dover dock continued to be busy with ships and men as he sat low in the passenger seat of Nichols's Jaguar. He'd finished a perimeter walk, meeting up with Lake and Olivar, pointing out Elias on the lounge's balcony. Preparations for this capture had taken the whole of the week since his return from Scotland. A great fuss for one woman, he thought, but he knew he wasn't privy to the whole case, not that he wanted to be, given the way Lake and Olivar had been barking at each other.

Taylor cupped his radio pinned to his coat, a new helmet on his lap. "They haven't spotted Hines yet," he told Nichols.

"He still has a few minutes." Nichols kept one hand on the wheel, watching passengers as they descended from the ferry under black clouds and beating rain. Their wheeled luggage bounced on the slatted ramp. "Elias was right. I should have taken him in earlier."

The phone rang. Nichols pulled it from its cradle.

"Bring her rucksack separately," Nichols said. "But you make sure it doesn't go missing. We've had enough things find legs."

Taylor set his hand on the door handle and readied himself for action. He scanned the area for Lake and Olivar among the constables gathering behind a police van. It was all Taylor could do to remain still until the order to proceed was given. Nichols leaned down in the driver's seat as three men and a woman stepped onto the gangway. Bulletproof vests bloated their chests. An east wind fluttered their sleeves.

The Jaguar's windscreen shattered. Glass spewed inward, slicing as blue-edged shards. Taylor ducked. Nichols shoved his door open and rolled under the car. Shots hit the hood. Taylor slid from the seat to the ground. He made the choice to rush toward the ship, slapping his helmet on his head and clicking the new-style fastener shut. The shots had separated him from Nichols. This was not part of the plan. This was an arrest of an unarmed woman, not an assault.

He was grateful that he wasn't carrying his heavy nightstick and torch. He sprinted as bullets pitted the asphalt at his feet. He dashed toward the safety of a cargo container. He kept as low as he could to avoid being shot.

Kitner's cries of "Cease fire" came from Taylor's radio.

Then Nichols's voice blared. "Get the woman."

Taylor's ear ached from all the noise. He peered around the container. The stink of the sea was strong as ever and floating above that stench, gunsmoke. Police whistles blasted. A half-dozen riot-clad officers bolted from concealment. They split up, firing, and moving toward the ferry.

He dashed for the boat, no shots coming his way. His breath shallow and his hands clammy, he narrowed his focus to the oval shape of the ferry's entrance. The running pained him, but he fought the aches in his body with a chant. "*Man-ches-ter U-nit-ed.*"

He recognized Lake on the gangway. Olivar preceded him. Bullets zinged into glass, cutting through the cloth-lined gangway and pounding into metal. He duck-walked with one hand on the steel railing, swaying on the buoyant plank. The spongy mats surprised him as he lurched the last steps into the ferry.

Lake slipped and bounced dangerously close to the edge of the ramp. Landing on his side, he scrambled to his knees as Taylor reached him. Olivar convulsed, his head snapped. A red stain sprouted on his camelhair coat as he staggered. The small man fell forward and knocked the woman onto her back. Her navy cap slipped from her head. Taylor recoiled at the sight of her sallow face and chestnut hair on the soaked walkway.

Lake brushed by, shouting for a doctor as Taylor stepped toward the woman. Water ran pink beneath her. This disturbed him as he grabbed Olivar's feet. Lake lifted the little cop by his shoulders. Taylor's right leg buckled with a sharp pain. He didn't have time to identify it. He hobbled as he and Lake rushed Olivar into the inner lounge.

They placed him face down on a red couch. He made no grunt or sound of pain. His brow seemed too smooth for a living man.

A blond man with insignia on his sleeves dropped the woman on the floor. She kicked at him, rocking in an effort to sit up.

Lake pulled her to her feet, his face close to hers. He clamped his hands under her arms, lifting her off her feet, shaking her. Her small body flopped in his great mitts, her jumpsuit fluttering.

Taylor pushed Lake hard, causing him to crash into

the couch. The woman hit the ground first. Lake rammed him, felling him. They became a heap of bodies and then unknown hands pulled them apart. The three sat apart, bodies propped against furniture. Their breaths popped visibly as they shout accusations, with Taylor getting in the first word, "You could have killed her."

Lake responded, "She rates killing."

"She's our only witness. Commander wants her alive."

"She's shite. You giving me orders, Sergeant?" Lake asked with both fists cocked.

The blond man knelt beside Taylor. "You're bleeding."

The man had an accent, not of the Metropolitan Police. He touched Taylor's face. Taylor had forgotten about the windscreen, how it sliced as it imploded. He patted his pockets for a handkerchief but found none.

The man said, "We weren't expecting gunfire."

Heather yelled at the blond man in a language Taylor didn't know. The blond man answered her quite coolly, shoving her against a wall, pointing to her legs and making it clear he was about to shackle them.

"There wasn't supposed to be any gunfire," Lake said. He grabbed Heather by the hair. "Look what you've done."

Not a question, so she didn't answer, though her mouth hung wide open. Her blue eyes dilated. Her body shuddered in the oversized uniform. She remained limp, waving her manacled wrists, beseeching Taylor. She struggled toward him. Her face had a lemon tinge, not an attractive glow. Her pink lips didn't curve up as Sorenson had drawn them. Fever-chapped and split, they lacked allure and spoke of long illness. He didn't embrace her. She alarmed him, with her wide eyes and lifted hands, swearing one minute and cuddling the next.

The blond man scooped her back into his arms. Taylor backed off, scouring the room for something to stop the bleeding from his leg. But before he could find anything, a star pattern of light blazed into the lounge. He stretched up to see over the railing, his eyes still dazzled.

A police launch nudged the ferry then lowered a connecting ramp with a slam. He wondered who ordered the launch. Was it a part of Nichols's plan? Maybe Elias wanted the woman more than he said? Perhaps Elias had come for her, come with his own police force? The blond man and his crew?

Hands lifted Olivar, cushion and all, onto the canvas slide, over the side to the waiting boat. Nobody asked Taylor to help, and they didn't help him. Maybe they didn't see him. He had a hard time seeing.

Lake followed after Olivar, the slide buoying with his weight. Heather and the blond man went next over the side. They slid with a grating sound, the shackles causing friction.

Taylor rose, but his legs splayed, his palms couldn't grip, and he hadn't strength to push up from the floor. He made fists as he slumped downward.

"Sergeant?" A woman's voice. Her touch on his neck frightened him. "Are you Sergeant Gareth Taylor?"

"Yes." He nodded, and that proved a very bad idea as black, blue, and red spots flashed in front of his eyes. His stomach cramped. He tilted his head up so he could examine the policewoman.

Her oval face had a narrow nose, freckles across it, and flecks of mascara at the corner of one of her brown eyes. He smiled at her, tried to stand, and clutched her shoulder. She stumbled, swayed, and their heads knocked. A policeman seized him about the waist. Together, they all wobbled into an upright position.

His weakness embarrassed him. They took no notice.

"You're wanted by the commander." She steadied herself. "He's in the ambulance on the dock. Can you manage?" Her policewoman's cap was askew and that was her only imperfection.

He almost laughed. Did he have a choice? The commander called.

They bumbled toward the vehicle. Splashing through small puddles, they helped him inside. He sprawled on the floor, puffing and noticing the shiny rips in his clothing and the boots of the medics.

One bent over Nichols, listening to his heart. Condensation beaded on the oxygen mask over Nichols's nose and mouth. Moisture beaded on the tubing and the trolley. Taylor sniffed and, among the medicinal smells in the ambulance, was the sea-soaked wool of his uniform.

He wondered how Nichols could have called for anyone, strapped as he was to the mobile bed with a gray blanket tucked about him. His eyes weren't even open.

Another medic ripped Taylor's pant leg. "Not bad. Glass. A few stitches'll get you back on your feet. Maybe not. What's this?"

Taylor didn't answer as his leg was probed. His mind drifted as pain gripped him.

The medic held him down. "Don't move," he said. "We've stopped the bleeding. Didn't you know you'd been shot?"

Taylor hadn't known. What he had known was that people were dead who were alive not an hour ago.

The medic gave him an ice pack for his face. The coldness stung and comforted as it muffled the noise of the rumbling tires beneath him.

"Your commander will live." The medic tapped his own chest. "Heart, you see. Ridiculous, a man in his condition rushing around in a commando raid."

"Wasn't a raid," Taylor said. "An arrest, that's all. One woman."

The medic asked him about other wounds. He shook his head. He didn't tell of Lake's freckled hands twisting the lapels of his uniform. There had to be some bruising. Lake didn't end up on the floor. He bumped against that bubbled wall.

Taylor sighed and hoped they all lived. He put his hands together as he felt a needle prick his skin, just one more pain in a day of misery.

Chapter 37

Elias

From the balcony of the dock's observation lounge, Elias gazed toward the circle of police vehicles in the Dover car park. Nearby the Rotterdam ferry lay at anchor, its decks emptied, and its flags snapping in the stiff breeze. This was the fourth hour since its arrival. All the passengers but one had cleared customs. That *one*, Heather Hiscocks, remained inside, a matron fitting her with a bulletproof vest.

Nichols had ordered him not to approach the ferry and not to mess with the arrest. He must stand down until the prisoner was secured.

"You'll have plenty of time to question her," Nichols said, at the bottom of the lounge stairs.

Elias had climbed them, his right hand in contact with the railing. Nichols went to his car.

What Nichols didn't say, friend that he was: that an elderly man, Elias, with a dicey heart and no gun, would be in the way. He would be a burden for the other officers and an obstacle should the takedown not go as planned.

He didn't plead, with Nichols turning away as more cars arrived. The sun made a poor effort to break through the thick clouds and illuminate the scene.

Elias didn't remind Nichols of the international implications of the case or the necessity for co-operation. No, he pulled two chairs from the lounge and sat with his feet up under the overhang, out of the rain.

Because, unlike Nichols, Elias needed Heather alive. He needed the account numbers she carried, the aliases she'd used, and the routes she'd traveled. He needed any name or scrap of name she could recall. So he'd agreed to watch rather than participate.

He wanted to make her suffer, to render her helpless, and then pry information from her while she was heavy with sleep, dizzy with fear, hungry, thirsty, and unwashed. He would tempt her with freedom, offer parole in exchange for names, dates, and accounts. Of course, he had no power to grant her any privileges, but she would not know this. She might know that she was being held under the Protection Against Terrorism Act and had no rights, no prerogatives and no access to counsel. But she would not feel her predicament until he got his grip on her life.

He stood and stretched, drumming on the railing to express his annoyance as the second hand ticked its way around the numbers on his watch face. He hummed the nursery rhyme, north, east, south, west. He knew police snipers hid behind each balcony or improvised barrier, waiting with their eyes to their sights. They had their orders: prevent any attacks on Heather Hiscocks, kill anyone who intervenes in the arrest. This was not the moment for restraint, hesitation, or mercy.

He heard the faint noises of Dover at midday. Unexpectedly, there came a tinny rattling of the sliding glass door behind him. The lounge's door scraped as it opened.

Two men argued as they entered. Sergeant Kitner stumbled into Elias, shoved by Brett. Elias saw the pleasure in his son's eyes. Brett loomed in his dark leather coat and matching boots.

Elias gripped the railing as Brett cornered him. Neither Kitner nor the distant snipers could protect Elias. The snipers might spot Brett, but how would they know to kill him? Would they ignore their primary objective, Heather Hiscocks, to execute an unknown?

Elias raised one hand, an ambiguous motion for prying eyes but not one which would alarm Brett.

"I'll go down for theft, even robbery," Kitner said. "But not murder." He shoved Elias against the wall. Kitner wore a black jumpsuit, wide web belt, bulletproof vest, radio, and heavy boots. Helmetless, he stood with arms outstretched. "Brett, we're here for the money. The girl, the money. That's it. Your father can wait."

"Isn't it right and proper a son should kill his father?" Brett let the door slam. "Isn't that the ancient way to power? Kill the father."

Brett put his left hand on Kitner's chest and watched Elias as he edged to the right. He took very small steps in his leather shoes. He didn't want to slip and fall in front of Brett. He didn't want to give Brett any additional advantage, like collapsing at his feet.

"In fairy tales, you idiot." Kitner drew his semi-automatic from its holster. "Think, man. Why we'd come here? We don't need to bother with him. We've kept him off the scent so far. I mean, how much do you want? There's millions. We get the Swiss account numbers from Heather, and we're home free."

Brett pointed at Elias. "He's not one to give up. He has honor, nobility, a soldier's ethic. He's has to go." He flicked his wrist. A silver blade became visible against his coat. "You should've seen him, down on his knees over Sorenson. He knew it was me, but he didn't tell anyone. He wanted to take me himself. Even now, Amsterdam's finest. Look at him. I want to see him twitch, beg. I want him down on his knees to me."

Kitner didn't look. "Hines said you'd try something like this." He kicked a chair, this time at Brett.

"Try?" Brett moved closer, bending his elbow to bring up the knife. He pushed Kitner and, with a thrusting twist, sliced at the side straps of his vest. Kitner jumped back.

The time and ferry now forgotten, Elias peeked around Kitner's shoulder. Sweat beaded on the back of Elias's neck. He stopped himself from glaring at his son, slowed his heart by setting his mind to calculate multiplication tables.

Gunshots cracked from the opposite rooftop, blasting Brett backward through the glass door. Elias gave thanks as Kitner pulled him down. They scrambled through the shattered door. More shots slammed into the brick facade. These Elias didn't expect. Who was the target now? Himself? Kitner?

Kitner took a rolling jump, allowing Elias to crawl behind a gold sofa, out of the sniper's line of fire. More glass broke. The fearful noise caused both of them to hide.

Kitner yelled into his radio, hand over his head. "Cease fire."

Elias stayed flat to the floor. He pulled his knees to his chest. He saw Kitner's hands and boots as he dragged Brett behind a green-patterned chair. Elias scuttled to his son, hearing no more shots.

"I'll call for an ambulance," Kitner whispered. "Keep him here. Keep low. I'm going to find out what's going on."

Elias shook his head at the gun that Kitner offered.

He placed it on the floor and sprinted for the stairs.

Tenderly, Elias brushed glass from Brett's hair. He tapped the insides of his son's palm as if it were made of electricity or fire. He studied the wounds, deep, precise, and fatal. He smoothed the coat over the body and closed his son's eyes, keening *"Unzen Vader in de hemelen, laot dienen name eheilegd worden."* The *Our Father*, it was his favorite prayer, with its pleas and its promises, our daily bread, and our temptations.

He didn't choke back on the words—the "forgive," or the "trespasses"—but pronounced them clearly, stroking Brett's unshaven cheek. Then he repeated it as if sealing a letter to heaven.

Chapter 38

Heather

From the purser's cabin, she endured the slow march topside with her hands cuffed in front of her and guards on either side, their arms linked with hers at the elbow. A bulletproof vest pressed tight to her chest, she smelled that lapping stench of the English seacoast, salt, seaweed, and algaed wood. Not the same bouquet as in Amsterdam, and not a welcoming aroma for a long-absent native. Neither was the pinging rain that the officers made certain hit her square in the face.

Escorted, she eyed the legs of the guards. Which could she reach with a kick? Should she spring and hit? Pretend to stumble then a jab to a guard's belly? They wouldn't be expecting that. Would it be worth the effort? How could she get off the boat? Jumping would put her where? In the water? But they were leading her to the dock, an ancient platform of stone, dotted with steel posts and hitches.

Her head ached from lack of sleep. Her body felt hot and cold. Yet, her tongue was dry. When did the purser give her tea? An hour ago? No watch to check. No silverware and no tray. He hadn't risked her getting any kind of weapon.

He'd handed her buttered toast and a peeled orange. "Just doing my job, miss." He smiled then. Now he seemed angry, directing others with nods of his head and quick waves of his hand. She hated him and planned to bite him before they separated.

She was annoyed by the baggy legs of the uniform she wore, by the thick-soled black shoes they'd given her, worn and too big, but she wasn't meeting the queen, just a magistrate and all his little helpers.

She stopped watching her shoes as she stepped onto the gangplank, felt its rippling wobble. The rain on her face stabbed.

The purser pulled her forward, his hand gripping the armhole of her vest. "This way."

She wondered at his urgency. Did he need to impress someone? Make a show of her detention? She peered at his face, chin down, rain beading on his nose and cheeks. He spoke into his radio, not commands but inquiries. Somebody nearby was monitoring their progress, somebody important, maybe behind the unloaded luggage, the containers, the cloth carts the porters were shoving about. She couldn't get away. The two guards behind her carried rifles.

She willed the gray, sad sky to snow and give a feathery dusting to line her way. Where was the herald to announce her captivity and to present this marvelous moment of being sent down? After all, she was being assigned a new place to live, a crowded house with locked doors and no sneaking out for a quick smoke.

A grip around the waist. What was this for? She didn't see who pulled her down. She was on her back on the dirty gangway mat with all the breath knocked out of her, her head ringing, and the cuffs cutting into her skin. A weight upon her proved too heavy to move. She tried to roll and kick. She heard shots, deafening shots.

Someone hauled her, great weight and all, back inside the ferry.

The purser dove to the floor and pulled a gun from an inside holster. He slid toward her, shielding his head with one hand, firing across her body into the open air.

Dirt and smoke smeared the purser's face and clothes.

Large hands lifted the weight from her chest. It was a small man, completely limp. Blood dripped, and she feared what it meant.

She got to her feet, one chance to get off this ferry.

"Get him into the lounge," the purser shouted.

Heather scrambled toward the stairs, but the purser tripped her. She kicked, but she was too slow. He rolled onto one knee, firing again.

Glass cracked, bounced off the warning signs and lock boxes. Booted feet ran. The purser kept a hand on Heather's vest as she crept toward the back of the boat. The cuffs made her movements awkward.

"Keep down," the purser yelled as he reloaded.

Heather kept moving, the lounge in sight. Fear choked her, yet this might be her chance to get into the water. Jump, then swim. Let them shoot each other. She'd cling to a post until nightfall, which came early in December. Then another man seized her, lifted her to eye level, and shook her back and forth until she nearly vomited. She drooped, a wet doll in his big hands. His eyes were blue, his black hair straight and his mouth stretched red with anger. Who was he? Was he trying to kill her?

His words cascaded threats, bottom teeth uneven. She understood this as a new danger, a hatred born out of all this shooting. But anger was a weapon that she could use. She must excite it in her captor. She must ignore the vest and force her diaphragm into action. She must hurl insults into this lout's face.

She twisted, but her feet were useless in the heavy shoes. Then a fall to the floor, two men arguing over her, the purser acting the peacemaker. She cursed them all.

The man held her at arm's length, and another man grabbed her legs. They carried her to the railing and dropped her. Sound erupted from her throat. She couldn't believe she was falling upside down onto a cloth ramp. Salt air stung her eyes. She tried to grip the edge, but it was too wide. Here was that old problem of being small. Far below her waves lapped, and an engine chugged. She formed another plan: hit with her cuffed hands.

As she landed, her head slammed into some body. She glimpsed black shirts, black buttons, and white faces. No one spoke nor showed concern. She'd been transferred, dumped off as somebody else's problem.

More hands upon her. These tossed her onto a different deck. Whose custody was she in? MI5, MI6, CIA? Let it not be the Americans. They'd subject her to psychological tests and truth drugs. She didn't want to be a lab rat in some scientist's ten-year study.

Men shoved her about like the old porters she'd seen on the dock. They dumped her onto a bunk by a chest and stepped away.

"Not her blood," one said.

She stared at her sleeves, smeared red and sticky.

Then he pressed a wet cloth over her nose and mouth. She punched upward with her cuffed fists, hitting nothing, and then hearing nothing. Her heart which had beaten against her chest with such fury slowed as if to cease completely. Black sleep swept through her, her limbs relaxing as if boneless.

Chapter 39

Taylor

In Nichols's hospital room, Taylor shivered as if from an inner cold which his uniform couldn't shield him. Maybe he'd developed a nervous tic. He'd been released with a pocketful of antibiotics, pain meds, and instructions for changing the dressings covering the stitches in his leg. He considered the wounds he'd be keeping and the time for their healing. First time for a forced vocation. First time, too, he'd had surgery with a day in recovery. They'd taken his watch, and there was not a clock in the room. It was odd not knowing the exact time and date.

Unease blanked words from his brain, or perhaps he was agitated by the unfriendly smell of ammonia and floor wax and those cream walls striped with afternoon shadows. He worried about Nichols's color, his weakness. There had been no improvement in either since the shooting.

Nichols remained in bed, though he wore his own pajamas now. Taylor tapped his notebook. Nichols opened his eyes.

"I'm to say that Captain van den Dolder has departed," Taylor said.

"That's for the best," Nichols said. "We wouldn't want a foreign national interfering with a police investigation." He pointed to the *Financial Times* on the bedside table. Taylor picked it up and offered it to him. His eyebrows arched, then he asked, "How's the leg?"

"Stiff." Taylor knocked on the wood armrest, holding back any mention of the pain that regularly shot through his calf. He told himself it was a twinge which would dissipate with exercise. "Stitches out in a week to ten days."

The surgeon ordered him to use crutches if he was determined to walk. Taylor had abandoned them at Nichols's door.

He had a lopsided gait but that, too, would diminish with time. Why, hadn't he walked almost normally the ten steps from that door to this chair? Neither the PC who held the door open, nor Nichols himself, had commented on his posture or effort. He bent toward Nichols, concentrating on moving smoothly. "You weren't caught in a crossfire, sir. You were targeted. I was targeted. Shots came from a single direction and shattered the windscreen. It was an attempt to blind us. But we were already in motion, seconds ahead of the impact."

Nichols folded back a page of the pink newspaper, lowering his glasses into place. No uniform, no honorary braid, and no insignia of his rank, he was naught but a small body in a faded dressing gown. He appeared to read. Taylor pressed on.

"Kitner wasn't with us at the ferry, nor at the ambulance, nor here at the hospital. We heard his voice over the radio, but no one saw him, except van den Dolder and that's when the shooting started. First, at van den Dolder and then you, me, Olivar, and Lake."

Beside him, Nichols clicked the monitor hooked to his index finger which charted his heart beat by beat. The black phone lay out of its cradle on the table.

"Men get separated in a fight," Nichols said. "I'd like tea."

"Two senior officers gone missing in the same week? Is no one looking for them? They're armed and dangerous, Hines especially."

Nichols showed no interest, He removed his glasses as he settled his head against the propped pillows and closed his eyes.

"Captain van den Dolder was looking for him," Taylor continued in a steady voice. "Or someone in Scotland. Standing in the rain, sir, the umbrella broke, and the local police arrived. Was that you who called them? Someone notified them of our inquiries."

Nichols opened one eye. "Wonderful imagination, Gareth." He looked at the flowers on the rollaway table. "Warrants have been issued for them. The one for Hines has been circulating since Glanz's murder. Elias's idea. I didn't agree with it. I was wrong. I had a wild idea Hines would leave the country on his own, save us the trouble of prosecuting him."

"During our visit to Scotland?" Taylor asked. "You gave Hines time for an escape?" He nodded with comprehension. "You never needed the girl, nor me. It was all for show. Hines told me at the warehouse. I never thought to believe him."

Nichols put the phone back in its cradle and watched it. The door opened, and Taylor moved to intercept. He pried himself from the chair by pushing off from the armrest. He hopped, one hand on the metal frame of the bed and met the constable at the door. He accepted a blue telegram from the guard's hand. It wouldn't be news he wanted to hear.

Nichols opened his eyes. "Read it, Taylor."

Taylor expected it to be from Elias—another death.

Nichols's voice was suddenly strong. "Out loud, Taylor."

Taylor reddened. "Dover. Fifteen December 1980. Jurg deported. Cash and cargo intercepted. Van."

He offered Nichols the telegram, but he rejected it, giving Taylor a disappointed grumble. He shifted his body on the two pillows at his back, white sheets folded back. "Read this," he said and patted the newspaper.

Taylor picked it up. "Commander Vernon Nichols of the London Metropolitan Police is in hospital after a drug seizure at Dover turned deadly. Several officers were wounded, including an American, who is not expected to live."

Taylor set the paper on the bed. "Olivar's dead."

Because of the girl, whom Lake nearly broke in half by shaking. Now she was locked in solitary, incommunicado, in Brixton.

Nichols sighed. "You lived. Hines never got to you."

Was that how he thought of the shooting at Dover? *He lived, I lived. Now we can both retire to the seaside and wait out Judgment Day.*

"He did get to me," Taylor said. "He and Kitner attacked me at the National Theatre, but beating a man to death is hard work, harder than Kitner expected. He wasn't good at it." He stared at Nichols. "Hines should at least pay for that."

"He'll pay." Nichols touched his chest, either in promise or in pain.

Taylor heard the heart monitor make a loud noise. He fretted as to its meaning. "Should I get the matron?"

"Calm yourself, Taylor," Nichols said. "I'm not dying. I'll live long enough to see this case to court."

"It'll be a whitewash, won't it?" Taylor puffed out

the words, giving the vowels volume and himself strength. "So the Met comes off clean."

Nichols stared at the ceiling. "Elias suspected government involvement, too much money for individuals to be handling. He's been on the case these last years, with Olivar."

"Smart man." Taylor's voice had an anguished grind.

Nichols's eyes closed. "A loss. You must understand."

"Olivar was killed with armor-piercing bullets." Taylor's lips quivered. He stared at his shoes to check his anger. "'Vengeance is mine, saith the *lord*.' Elias said it over and over again, in Edinburgh, after our room has been slashed. I looked it up." He edged forward. "Romans Twelve, Nineteen. 'Beloved, never avenge yourselves, but leave it to the wrath of God; for it is written, Vengeance is mine: I will repay, saith the Lord'"

"You can't know. Elias has a mission," Nichols said. "He loves his country, wants to restore Amsterdam to its glory days. Impossible, but you never saw the ruins the Germans and then the British and the Americans made of Holland."

Taylor lowered himself into the chair. Standing pained him. Nichols had used him. The commander had subjected him to the bruising by Hines and Kitner, the cold of Scotland, and the shooting at Dover.

"Then the drugs. They ruined his Amsterdam. He fought a world war and came home to heroin bars." Nichols tipped his chin down. "Hard to hate the country you love."

"Olivar's dead." Taylor put both hands on the bed. "Evan's injured. You're injured. Your wife and son are in hiding. Suzanne Cooper's gone missing," he whispered to Nichols as if that would stir him to weep. "I've been posted, sir. Southwark is sending me down."

"Wales?" Nichols asked, sweat beading on his brow.

"Yes, sir," he said. "The DCI called me in this morning."

"Lovely country." Nichols spoke without energy.

Taylor reached to take Nichols's pulse. "Must I go?"

"You must go, Sergeant." Nichols batted his doe-eyes, his face bright, and his shoulders taut. "You must smile all the way there."

Taylor didn't like this development.

Nichols said, "'Elias, prophet come to judge, Yahweh is God." He sat up, raising his hands in prayer. "He has chosen another to lead his children through the raging storm. He has set His mark upon His champion, and none may hinder the work of the Lord.'"

Taylor yelled for the PC guarding the door. "Get matron. Quick, man. He's raving."

He held the door open, balancing on his good leg, willing the hallway to fill with medical personnel to save his commander.

"Taylor, you needn't shout." Jean Nichols patted his arm as she entered. She kissed Nichols, taking his outstretched hand in hers.

"Mrs. Nichols?" Taylor staggered. "But you're—"

"Fine, Taylor," She smiled. "Thank you for asking. Vernon?"

"Jean, dear," Nichols said. "Taylor's just leaving."

She turned her head, calm and smiling, as if she'd returned from the shops and not from hiding.

Taylor felt his surprise subside. He released the breath he didn't realize he was holding. His brain sped up even as his heart slowed. If Mrs. Nichols was here, then the threat to Nichols had ended. Kitner must be in custody and Heather Hiscocks a liability. It would never come to trial, and a trial was all that would save her, ill as she was.

So now Taylor saw his situation clearly—how, while he had been recovering, morphine numbing him, the Metropolitan Police had been busy, securing the murderers, suppressing evidence, and transferring him. He'd served his purpose, drawn out Hines and Kitner, ferried Evan to Scotland, and squired van den Dolder around Edinburgh.

At Dover Taylor had played the brute at the ferry, an extra pair of hands to carry Olivar's limp body out of the line of fire. Now he'd be sent down to Wales and dog catching, drunks and druggies to waltz into the cells.

He stumbled with the shock of it all. His leg muscles contracted and pain spun up through his gut. He braced himself on the arm of the chair behind him. Two days to lose touch with the case. Doped and made stupid by drugs, he felt humiliated. Here he had been rabbiting on about Hines and Olivar while Nichols sat there knowing all about it. He didn't care what was written in the newspapers or Elias's telegram. It was old news to Nichols. He probably had Hines in custody and Kitner typing out his confession minus his part in Taylor's beating. Didn't want his mates to know that he laid fists on a fellow copper.

Mrs. Nichols smiled at him so brightly that it unnerved him. She knew more than he ever would. He saw Mrs. Nichols's smile not as pleasure or delight in seeing her husband improved in health, but as an imperial munificence. He, Taylor, had been touched and blessed by imperial whim. If he kept still and silent in the dreary realm of Wales, he would, in time, return as Mrs. Nicholas had returned, in triumph to the capital.

A buzz went through his face, a prickling of unknown origin. It hurt him as her smile had hurt him. It forced him from the room, down the halls, and out the double glass doors to the street. The cold air couldn't blister him nor the rain discourage him. He found his old power to disregard injury and concentrate on one thought: protect the girl. He must keep her from harm and keep the truth from dying with her as part of it had died with Olivar.

Maybe Taylor was out of his depth, a blind plod as Hines thought. Maybe he should take up dog catching. But not today. Today it was Taylor to the rescue, Taylor the mighty, the Southwark savior. He had to be quick, quicker than Hines, than Elias or Kitner or Nichols. Or Heather would be nothing but a smear of blood on a cell floor.

"Wales, it is. Wales and dog catching. That's the life for me." He hobbled on his bandaged leg, his face grim with pain. He'd been warned not to stress the limb. The wound could reopen, and he'd be back on the surgeon's table, a prime candidate for complications and infections.

Outside the hospital, he hailed a taxi, slid in, and gripped the inside door handle with strength enough to distract his mind from his injury. As to the matter of disobeying his doctors and defying his superiors…well, how many times could one be sacked?

Chapter 40

Elias

In a deluxe cabin in the Amsterdam-bound ferry, Adjutant Beers, still dressed in the purser's uniform, handcuffed Peter Jurg to the bedpost. All the rushed-days that had gone by and this was the moment Beers and Elias reunited, at journey's end.

"Once we're at sea, the buffet will open, and I'll bring you some supper," Beers said. He offered him the small key to the cuffs. Elias accepted it, gave Beers a smile, and dismissed him.

He draped Jurg's coat over the edge of the bunk and eyed their luggage piled there. Jurg slouched, twisting his wrist against the cuff, and banging the chain. His brow was very red where the sweat beaded. He'd been pumped with morphine to ease the withdrawal, but Elias didn't know if Jurg had received any today. He growled and groaned and called Elias names out of Trotsky: running dog, bourgeois swine.

Elias touched his temple as pain shot from his eyes to the back of his head. A new pain. He'd have to tell his doctor about it. He slumped onto the opposite bed. The key bounced on the tightly-tucked cover.

His left arm throbbed. He tried to turn it, but it disobeyed him, remaining flat on the wool blanket. He couldn't see his watch and didn't know how much time has passed. He felt troubled about this and about his numb fingers and twitching toes.

Jurg stood, his chain stretched. "What's wrong with you?"

"It wasn't me," Elias said. "I didn't pull the trigger, Alise."

What a place to think of one's dead wife? If his knees would hold him up, he would pray for her. Forgiveness, wasn't that what one gave the dead or begged from them?

He'd give Brett a burial, far from Alise. She would not have to sleep with a criminal 'til Judgment Day, not with a killer of women and girls. Her own son put a gun to his father's heart on the Dover dock. That same father stalked his son for the good of the state. That son's death had been sanctified by the Dutch government, a clean, swift end to a disturbed relation.

Jurg kicked the steel door. "Get me out of here."

Aroused, Elias sat up, his feet on the floor. He wished for sleep, healing rest, and silence. He worried about the noise Jurg was making. Some might accuse him of torture as Jurg's voice rose shrill in a bolted cabin with it one small window.

Elias couldn't see the dock as the ferry departed. He heard the plowing of the boat and smiled. He tried to remove his shoes, but his hands flopped against his knees.

"Pray with me, my brother," he said for the third time as his tongue knocked the insides his mouth. The words, unformed, bulked up like clotted cream.

He saw Brett before him, not Jurg in his gray

jumpsuit. The cabin vanished, and Brett loafed before Elias, fearless, outside the post office on Singel Road, outlined by the rising sun. Brett counted dollars into a young girl's hands, the runner Elias and Beers had trailed from Oosterpark.

Beers snapped pictures of the exchange, a photo of Brett and the girl, then some of each: Brett in his favorite leather jacket and brown boots, so smartly polished, the girl, in Levis with her hair hidden under a bandana.

Windows had opened above them. Amsterdam awoke. Bodies had edged out of doors to snatch newspapers or bottles of milk. Smugglers had dashed between crossing trams.

That was Holland, sinking—the great sea power, defeater of the Spanish and defender of the Jews, nothing but some slippery cheat plying children with sticky dreams of good times and brilliant fun.

Elias's glasses slipped farther down his nose, His jaw slackened uncontrollably. His heart jumped with small cursed painful leaps against his ribs. His eyelids twitched as his head hit the bed. His right arm jerked beneath him. He couldn't make it stop. The arm grew shorter in his sight as did the orange stripe of the blanket. He had a foreshortened view of the cabin and of Jurg.

He heard a clank of chain: Jurg on his knees, fingers stretched toward the doorknob. Jurg's mouth was full of shapes and noise, but he was not praying.

Hot crackling breaths pinged in Elias's lungs. He counted them and the time between them: uneven, harsh. They cut his chances of getting home and of making tea in the yellow teapot. The rabbits would eat the cabbages in his garden. The sparrows would nest in his hedge. The sunflowers would forget to bloom without his watering, and all the roses would droop.

His chest sank, softening like wet linen, faltering like white morning light giving way to gray rain. His ears bled. Then his heart stopped.

Chapter 41

Heather

In her solitary cell, the metal door squealed. Heather crawled away from it and from the knotted thoughts of yesterday—those plinks and thunks in wood; rifle shots; an officer falling, pinning her to the ship's deck, his last breath in her ear. The sight of his dark hair impressed her before the air went out of her.

She dreaded whoever approached her—a man from his heavy steps—but he didn't speak, and her swollen eyes couldn't give her a clear picture of him. She hated her fatigue. Twenty hours without Marta's drops to break the fever.

The looming, bobbing shape enveloped her.

She balled up her fists to strike at the big man who lifted her. He cradled her, terrifying her with his green-glowing eyes in his bleached-cloud face. His loping run shook her every bone. His wool shirt and brass buttons scratched her face.

She made croaking and bubbling noises. Her urgent sounds were muted by his thick clothes. She ceased

struggling and let her bare feet dangle. Her face was
stroked by a wet cloth as he tucked her between starched
sheets on a hard bed. Her brain registered a flickering image of a white room and of torsos in white coats. Her ears
recorded some talk above her, about being all right now.
There followed mutterings about low blood pressure,
about Wales and America, a tailor, and Sorenson. Then
warm cloths dabbed her face and hair, relieving those surfaces of blood, dirt, and grease.

The glow of light on her face eased her cough,
stilling her fears. Her knees relaxed. Her head sank back
on the pillow. Her eyes fluttered open, and she began to
distinguish the busy people in the room.

A pat on her hand, the big man who carried her
smiled at her, his knees close together in the plastic chair.
He held her hand between his, fingers flat, like her grand-
father used to, greeting women at church fetes. It was an
old-fashioned gesture and gentle. She remembered him
from the ferry. She'd been grateful when he'd stopped
that other policeman from shaking her to pieces.

"I'm Sergeant Gareth Taylor, and you're in the infirmary," he said. "You're safe now. They'll take care of
you here." He pointed to the far corner of the ceiling. A
white camera hung there, its lens shiny. "Guards know
where you are, but they won't trouble you while under
medical care."

She nodded and waited for the really bad news.

"You're being held under the PATA," he said to-
wards her ear, not whispering but confidential. "Protection Against Terrorism Act. No solicitor will come. Your
family won't come."

*What else? Out with it. There's more or else you
wouldn't have pulled up a chair.* She saw it his eyes.
"And?" she asked.

"And you can be held indefinitely," he said. "And you may be."

The fate she'd willed for another, for Brett. She coughed, felt thirst, and realized the little strength she gained from medical care was ebbing. She checked her belligerence. "You were sent to tell me this?"

He blinked and rubbed his hands with vigor. "No. No one knows I'm here." There was pain in his cream-colored face. "When they figure it out, they'll come for me. I'm being sent down."

She didn't ask any more questions.

"So." He smiled and folded his hands. "If you want to get a message to someone, I could pass it on," he said. "I'll be passing a number of postboxes." He arched his eyebrows. His face seemed less pale. "I'm not on the case anymore."

"The case?" she croaked out. She wanted to ask more, about Sorenson, Brett, and Willem, but her coughing stopped her.

He didn't seem bothered by it. He even offered to pat her back. He pointed with the index finger of his left hand. "You banked the money that went missing. Millions have gone missing, you see. And they, Scotland Yard, Bank of England, Barclays, think you know where it is. They believe you do, and they want you to help them recover it."

"Millions?" She coughed again and thought, *A hundred thousand maybe, not millions like he means millions*. She made the deposits and remembered the numbers. That was why she came after Sorenson. The numbers hadn't tallied. Someone was stealing, skimming. But it wasn't Sorenson. She knew that now. It was some nameless Brit. How about that. Still, that might be her trump card, keeping the big banks guessing.

"Has to be you." Taylor smiled. "You're the rogue

element, the criminal genius. They're the establishment, and they're embarrassed. You outwitted them. You stole money using a computer, and you could do it again. They haven't learned how to stop you."

He winked. She winked back.

He waited while the matron helped her to drink a glass of orange juice. She sipped more juice and shifted in the bed as she was informed that she was dehydrated and running a fever. She needed rest and nourishment and not someone keeping her awake.

The matron frowned at Taylor. "Five more minutes."

"A Yank, Olivar, understood your *work*," Taylor said. "You did something new. Maybe not you by your-self, I don't know. They want you to tell them about it." He paused, eyes wide. "And whatever is sickening you won't stop on its own."

"And if they shut me away, I die," she said in spurts. "Everybody gets a raise and keeps their pensions."

She grew agitated by the crisp sheets. She willed the matron to disappear. The gaunt woman gave them five more minutes. What could she get in five more minutes?

"Exactly." He released her hand. "You can bargain with them. That I do know."

She tamped down her suspicions. "You'll help me?"

He sat back, stretched out one leg, and rubbed it. "I've done all I can by bringing you here." The creak of metal as the chair bore his full weight, not fat, not old, and not much older than she. Hurt, too. He winced and squirmed as if telling her: "You don't have to believe me. I wouldn't believe me. Lies, everybody lies."

He gazed around at the other, empty beds and the matron.

She wished she could believe him. "The man who fell on me?" she asked, squeezing her cup, concentrating on each word.

"Dead," he said, his lips tight. "With armor-piercing bullets. They might have been aiming for you, miss, but I think they were aiming for him. He'd compiled evidence that implicated his superiors. That's a death sentence and no mistake."

He touched the corner of his left eye. She regarded his ruddy face, his thick clothes, and stillness. She registered the comfort he affected. She knew this was the last she would see of him. She ran her finger through her hair, a nervous habit.

"His name was José Olivar. Mean anything to you?" he asked, eyes focused on her, the policeman again, not the confidant.

She shook her head, pushed herself upright as a fit of coughing started. He put an arm around her and helped her drink.

"Emile Glanz?" Taylor asked. "Brett van den Dolder?"

She flinched and drank again.

"You knew him? Bad guy?"

"Threatened me." Her voice squeaked. Her hand trembled, so she set the glass on the side table. "In Zurich, Amsterdam."

"He wasn't alone in that," he said. "It's a big case, years old. The States are involved, and that's never good for England. My opinion."

That made her laugh. She pulled the sheet over her mouth as the coughing racked her. But the matron was far away and didn't hear her, so she didn't stop their conversation.

"I can get the matron." He wanted to help her.

She waved wildly at him with one hand. Ordinarily, a man that large would worry her, seeing him on the street, or passing him in a park, but here, beside him, she didn't feel fear. She felt protected, and sheltered.

He looked sideways as if even he couldn't face the truth he was telling. "They're all dead, the men I mentioned. One killed one right after the other. And there's art still missing. That was Olivar's part in the case. I was the blind dog in the corner everyone kicks."

She frantically signaled, "Don't make me laugh." All the silly gesturing sparked his laughter. He gripped his jaw, grimacing.

What a pair, the maimed and the mute.

The door opened. She expected the doctor. She kicked at the bedclothes and heaved herself left and right, utterly frightened by the shape that filled the doorway. He'd come for her that man who shook her on the boat, the one who nearly killed her with his bare hands.

Taylor caught her as she slipped from the bed. His voice was calm. "He's not here for you." His arm enclosed her. "He's here for me."

"That I am," Lake said. "So we'll be off then?"

He drew no closer. He crossed his hands in front of him, gloved and still. This interview was over with no wrenching good-byes. A nod, a shrug, and a turning away ended their entire association forever.

The door clicked closed. Her body grew cold and she inconsolable. She pulled all the bedclothes around her tight, her back pressed against the steel bedframe. She watched the twilight become darkness and wondered when the questioning by other officers would begin.

What would she say? Her story? Would anyone listen?

She'd draw. With her small hands, she'd etch into every inch of her cell wall images bold and mythic. She'd carve a tale of death and corruption, lovers parted, and heroes failing.

She'd work with plate, spoon, or cup edge, wrenching a story out of stone. Braced by one arm, straining upward to reach the topmost corners of her cell, she'd work the walls until they, her keepers, relented and gave her paper, pen, and ink. Thus she would damn them all, and they wouldn't be able to prevent her unless they burned down the jail.

Chapter 42

Taylor

As they reached the last checkpoint of the Brixton gaol, the duty sergeant handed Lake a heavy coat. "Commander thought you'd be wanting this."

Lake handed it to Taylor who received it with grateful surprise, expressing his thanks. He realized that Lake had brought it from the hospital and that Lake had spoken with Nichols. Lake had volunteered to collect him and to get him to Wales.

Taylor fumbled with the coat's buttons, flipping up the collar against the December evening's blast. Outside a panda car and driver awaited them. Lake held the back door open, ordering him in.

In Taylor's bedsit, Lake settled himself in the desk chair.

Taylor stood on the thin carpet beside his bed and gazed left to the window and right to the door. He'd never had guests here. It wasn't a place for guests. "What do I take?" he asked Lake as if banishment had rules, and Taylor didn't dare make a cock-up of his exile.

He fought the clenching pain that burned between his ribs, surprised that the corrosive acid didn't erupt through his skin and shred his uniform.

Lake winked. "What every warrior takes into the wilderness: clean shirts, clean socks, clean drawers, and your everlasting soul."

Taylor stared into the corner where his guitar stood. A cold twitch seized him as he surveyed all he must leave behind.

"Take it if it gives you comfort." Lake stretched and grabbed the guitar by its neck. He tucked it under his arm and plucked the strings.

Taylor didn't move. "Will they know? The Welsh officers?"

"As soon as you open your mouth, they'll know." Lake tuned the instrument. "But you're bigger than all of them put together, so I wouldn't worry. Knock a few heads together, and they'll leave off."

He set down the guitar to dial the phone. Taylor emptied his wardrobe, cramming the clothes in two suitcases. In the washroom, he removed his uniform and donned jeans, a jersey, and trainers. He swept the contents of his medicine cabinet into a sports bag and slung the bag over his right shoulder as he returned to the bedroom. He took no final survey of his flat. The packing he left to whichever constable had the bad luck to be assigned the duty. He forsook the contents of the bedsit. He would buy new things in whatever Welsh village claimed him.

But one question burned his lips: where was Suzanne Cooper? He had to wait before expelling the words. Lake held the telephone receiver to his ear then gave a pleased "Yes, yes," a joyful blurt as he hung up the phone.

Taylor wondered what news could make Lake happy. "Good news?" he asked. "Suzanne Cooper?"

Lake shook his head. "Commander's been sent home." His voice turned sharp. "You're not still thinking about her? She's not a priority."

Taylor shifted the bag higher on his shoulder. "Olivar promised he'd find her. He thought she was a priority."

"Olivar didn't find her," Lake said. "She's gone."

"Oliver is gone. Your partner is gone," Taylor growled out. His hands formed fists. He felt his chest swell.

Lake stared at him. "I don't need reminding." He shifted his shoulders in his great coat as if loosing up for a wrestling match.

They both exhaled heavily out their noses.

Taylor saw his breath and realized how cold the room must be. He wondered why Lake hadn't lit the gas fire. Too late to bother now.

He decided not to rile Lake further. He pulled open the drawer of his bedside table and retrieved his passport, abandoning everything else. He heard Lake open the door and saw the stairs looming before him.

Lake helped him with his bags. They dumped his luggage in the boot of the panda car, and off they sped to the railway station.

Taylor shook hands with Lake a second time, his luggage at his feet, the sport bag over his shoulder. He boarded the train and realized he'd forgotten to ask about his mates at Southwark. He couldn't believe he'd forgotten about Southwark.

ლაც

At the entrance to Conwy Castle, Taylor stopped short. It was not the thickness of the Easter Monday crowd that halted him but the young man who lounged against the towering wall, his two hands upon the knob of a walking stick. A man he hadn't seen in four months.

The sea breeze which stirred the hair and clothes of every tourist and passerby did not touch Evan Nichols where he stood in the crook of the rough structure.

Taylor shook Evan's hand, bending, smiling, delighted. His hand was still warm from the gloves that he had stuffed into the pocket of his leather jacket. Evan had a chastened look, a pinch to the skin between his eyes. There gleamed a whiteness underneath as if the skin had thinned from rubbing. Taylor wanted to take him by the chin and examine his face, which had been so broken when last Taylor saw it. He regarded the cane and felt he could ask about it.

Evan tapped the pavement with the silver-headed stick. "I don't need it. I carry it to annoy Dad. He's very sensitive about my injuries."

"As any father would be." Taylor flattened himself against the wall as he was nudged by a little boy in a pea coat. The lad regarded him with eyes rife with disbelief then poked him with empirical curiosity. The incident gave him an obvious reason to laugh, with no reference to Evan's visit or to the pleasure of not being forgotten in his place of banishment. He reached to shake the wee laddie's hand, but his mother collected the child just then with evident embarrassment.

"I wanted to thank you." Evan looked first up into Taylor's face then down at his own shoes. "I don't think that happens to you very often, but you tried to save my life. You did save my life if what my father says is true. He told me about Suzanne Cooper, told me everything. I didn't take it well, you can imagine."

"I have imagined it." Taylor's eyes were on the lengthening queue before the castle's entrance. "Not much to do around here but imagine."

"It is an odd country, isn't it?" Evan put on his gloves. "Cold nine days out of ten, raining when it isn't snowing, bleak and beautiful, a strange prize for a prince."

Taylor nodded his agreement. He'd taken an interest in Wales. He'd read all the guidebooks and local brochures.

The pictures confounded him though, with their perfect, unchanging record of countryside and town.

"Dad's retiring, you know that?" Evan's voice grew urgent. "You could be called back."

Taylor didn't answer. He didn't need hope.

"Dad said he recommended it. He said you were a good cop. You deserved a promotion." Evan shifted his walking stick from hand to hand. "He said you looked for Suzanne, that you were the only one who cared about her and wanted to find her."

Taylor frowned. "I didn't find her. I'm afraid no one will find her."

"Yes. I don't know how to accept that."

Now was the time for the "chin-up" speech: *My boy, my boy, love makes life a wonder and a wreck. Write a poem or a play if you can't get over a woman. Then plunge in again into that sea of feeling. You won't get jilted every time. There's plenty to enjoy, relish even.*

Taylor adjusted his hat and smoothed his coat collar that the wind had disturbed. He dispensed neither wisdom nor judgment, just indicated the ramparts behind them. "Seen the castle?"

"Many times," Evan said. "We holidayed here every summer."

"Then come and tell me what's changed," Taylor said. "So I can dazzle visitors with names and dates."

The two men passed through the castle's turnstile and descended the worn stairs. Taylor shortened his stride to keep pace with the smaller man through the roofless ruin.

End

About the Author

Deirdre Feehan is a writer, librarian, and native of California. She traveled extensively in Europe and resided in London for a time. She completed the UCLA's Writer's program in 2009, specializing in fiction. Her recent work includes an essay on Sir Carol Reed for the Senses of Cinema database; a photographically illustrated children's book, *ABC* starring Teddy and his friends; short stories in magazines and online 'zines; and two poems, "Orpheus & Eurydice: Two letters," in the online journal, *Slow Trains*. Feehan received honorable mentions in the 2015 Soul-Making Keats Literary Competition for her unpublished novel, *Aldo's Resume* and in the 2015 Ultra-Short Competition sponsored by The Binnacle at The University of Maine at Machias. *Taylor on Loan* is her first foray into crime fiction.

89880694R00146

Made in the USA
San Bernardino, CA
02 October 2018